FATAL MISTAKE

FATAL MISTAKE

THE UNBELIEVABLE MR. BROWNSTONE™ BOOK ELEVEN

MICHAEL ANDERLE

Fatal Mistake (this book) is a work of fiction. All of the characters, organizations, and events portrayed in this novel are either products of the author's imagination or are used fictitiously. Sometimes both.

Cover by Andrew Dobell, www.creativeedgestudios.co.uk

A Michael Anderle Production

LMBPN Publishing
PMB 196, 2540 South Maryland Pkwy
Las Vegas, NV 89109

First US edition, September 2018
Version 1.02 November 2020

FATAL MISTAKE TEAM

Special Thanks
to Mike Ross
for BBQ Consulting
Jessie Rae's BBQ - Las Vegas, NV

Thanks to the JIT Readers

James Caplan
Kelly O'Donnell
Mary Morris
Keith Verret
John Ashmore
Paul Westman
Daniel Weigert
Angel LaVey
Micky Cocker
Larry Omans

If I've missed anyone, please let me know!

Editor
Lynne Stiegler

To Family, Friends and
Those Who Love
to Read.
May We All Enjoy Grace
to Live the Life We Are
Called.

1

Major Davies looked up at the sky with a smile. Dark clouds blocked the moon and stars, and a torrent might start any minute. Bad weather would cut down on visibility, which would only benefit his team. The closer they could get without being spotted, the harder it would be for their targets to rally their defenses.

Someone up there wants us to kick a little ass for the good old USA.

Light chatter filled the clearing as the soldiers performed their final checks on their weapons and equipment. Men cleared chambers and slapped magazines into their rifles. A couple of men verified the charging status of their railguns. Others tapped away at the control pads on their wrists to verify the operational status of their tactical exoskeletons.

The major liked the new tech, expensive as it was. It didn't require him to do anything fancy. He could simply run and jump like normal. The enhanced strength allowed them to wear full armor without tiring, not just a bulletproof vest.

Faster, stronger, and safer. They could haul heavier weapons without vehicle support. Nice little bonus for any soldier, especially considering the dangerous enemies they were about to fight.

Going to show those terrorist bastards what it's like to have the US Army give them a proctology exam.

The major glanced down at the anti-magic deflector hanging around his neck. From what he'd been told, the crystals couldn't be underneath their armor and wouldn't interfere with their exoskeletons, but he didn't like having to rely on magical tricks.

It didn't matter what he preferred, though. That was just the world they lived in now.

He glanced down at his rifle.

Running all anti-magic rounds. This might end up being one of the most expensive small-squad raids in Army history.

Major Davies chuckled at the thought. He couldn't put a price on the safety of the United States.

Another soldier looked up from his rifle and smiled at the officer. "How are your wife and your new daughter doing, sir? What is her name again?"

"They're fine, Sergeant. And my daughter's name is Emily."

The sergeant nodded. "Surprised you didn't take some time off."

The officer chuckled and shook his head. "It's because I have a new kid that I *didn't* want to take time off."

Sergeant Jeffries grinned. "What, don't like the crying? Wanted to wait until she's sleeping better?"

"Nope, nothing like that. It's just, having a kid reminded me of why I joined the Army. Reminded me of the important things out there I need to protect. I went through the same thing when my son was born."

The other man's smile faded, and he gave a slow nod. "I know what you mean. When my son was born last year, it put a lot of this shit into perspective. It's his first birthday next week, and my wife's going all out."

Major Davies laughed. "My wife did that for our first kid. I told her it wasn't like he'd remember, so she told me she was going to go even crazier for our daughter's first birthday to force her to remember when she's older."

The sergeant shrugged. "At least you have some time to prepare yourself. A year's a long time."

A man and a woman approached, both in dark suits with wand holsters hanging from their belts.

Major Davies kept himself from frowning. The Paranormal Defense agents had been nothing but professional, and he was grateful to have active magical support. He just wished the DoD would hurry up and better integrate active magical beings directly into the military. They couldn't keep fighting their battles using old tactics and strategies, or constantly be borrowing resources from non-DoD departments.

The male agent nodded to Davies. "All our people are ready, Major."

He nodded back. "We should get ready to roll." He cleared his throat before speaking to the troops. "Everyone saddle up. I shouldn't need to remind you that our targets are extremely dangerous. Our rules of engagement are clear. We will breach the compound, and we will terminate every terrorist sonofabitch we run into."

He grabbed his helmet from the back of his exoskeleton. "Let's show these assholes that they can't do whatever the fuck they want just because they know a little magic."

The gathered soldiers yelled a loud chorus of "*Hooah*."

The major slapped on his helmet, and a second later the augmented reality heads-up display popped onto the front of his visor.

"This is Hammer 1," he transmitted. "Eagle 1 and Salt 1, do you read?"

"This is Eagle 1. Five by five."

"Salt 1. Five by five."

Major Davies started toward the edge of the clearing, the massive oak trees looming over him. The exoskeleton-clad Special Forces operators fell in behind him, two squads of six. Each squad contained four Special Forces operators and two magic users from the Paranormal Defense Agency. Eagle 1 and Salt 1 were comprised of other officers who helped provide tactical support from a field tactical center they'd set up about ten miles away.

No one wanted to risk drones spoiling their surprise party, so for now, the teams' support personnel were depending on helmet cams and vital readings for their understanding of the tactical situation on the ground. Even close air support was too risky, given the powerful and magical nature of their enemies. Chaff and flares didn't stop fireballs.

The teams left the clearing and entered the forest. The tall trees swayed lightly in the wind.

"This is Hammer 1. Engage night-vision mode."

An eerie green highlighted the trees and owls watching the marching operators.

I wonder if any of those birds work for the terrorists? These days you can never tell what's up. Fucking magic.

"Hammer 5, what do you got for me?"

The wizard took a few seconds to respond. "There's been no change in any of the warning magic. We've maintained surprise, Hammer 1."

"Let's pick up the pace, people, before the terrorists leave the compound because they're bored." The major's brisk walk turned into a jog, fallen branches crunching under the exoskeleton's feet.

They'd have to keep it reasonable. The witches and wizards couldn't keep up with them if they started sprinting at full speed, and they needed to have the flashy magic for the coming battle. Anti-magic deflectors might help close the gap between the normal humans and the magic-using terrorists, but there were a lot of unusual spells they might encounter.

Several minutes later the forest began to thin, revealing a nearby fence and a complex of buildings. Most were one story, but a few taller.

Almost time for the fun to begin.

The major smiled. The target site used to be the official corporate campus of a big tech company that had made a shitload of money back in the day, but they'd failed to pivot smartly once magic came back into the world. They'd unloaded the buildings to an interested private party who allegedly just wanted it for corporate team-building retreats, but FBI, NSA, and PDA investigators had learned that the little corporate retreat was something far more sinister.

Yeah. Just nice and normal, which is why our satellite and high-altitude recon coverage spotted roving guards and more than a few weird-looking creatures. Awful lot of magical security if this is just some place to do boring team-building shit.

According to his briefing, it was housing terrorists associated with a recent museum heist in LA. If it hadn't been for James Brownstone, practically a walking platoon by himself, the terrorists would have escaped with all the artifacts. He didn't know much about their motives, only that he'd been told they were associated with something called "the Council," which was some sort of terrorist group.

The major didn't give a shit who they were or about the particulars of their ideology. People who fucked with the country got put down. Simple as that.

He'd sworn an oath to defend his country against all enemies, foreign and domestic. There was nothing in there about exceptions because the bad guys happened to use magic.

"Detecting magic, Hammer 1," Hammer 5 reported.

"Everyone halt," Major Davies ordered. The soldiers and agents stopped and raised their weapons and wands.

"It's detection magic," explained Hammer 5. "Passive field. They don't know we're here yet. We should be able to take it out, but there's a risk that they'll sense what we're doing."

"We all expected this. Doesn't matter. We're damn close now." The major nodded. "Hammers 5 and 6 and Salt 5 and

6, clear it out. Everyone else, hold position until Hammer 5 gives the all-clear."

The witches and wizards raised their wands, murmuring incantations and gesturing precisely. A shimmering curtain of energy appeared a few yards in front of them, and after a few seconds, a gap appeared.

"All clear for about ten yards on either side," Hammer 5 reported.

We're coming for you, Council.

The teams moved forward. With the first magical barrier defeated, a far more conventional fence waited to thwart them next, but there were no sentries in the immediate area.

Too cocky for your own damned good. It's not like some punk mercs are coming for you.

"Hammer 2, prepare to open that up," Major Davies ordered. "Once we're through that fence, we should expect heavy resistance. Trust your training and equipment no matter what you see."

Hammer 2 jogged toward the fence and grabbed a pair of wire cutters from his tactical harness. Sometimes the simplest solution was the best.

Major Davies took a deep breath and raised his weapon. "Everyone prepare for breach. Let's kill ourselves a few magical terrorists."

No. Not good. This recipe is shit. Five stars? Who the fuck would give something with these ingredients five stars? Do they have no taste buds?

James stared down at his phone as he thumbed through barbeque recipes. The rest of the men from the Brownstone Agency milled around their tent. It'd been a long day of cooking barbeque for the competition. Now that night had fallen, most of the crowd was gone, but the PFW team still hadn't heard the results from the judges. It was taking them an unusually long time to deliberate, and James wasn't sure if that was good or bad.

He sighed. Whatever happened that night didn't change what the Brownstone Agency barbeque team needed to do in the future.

We need to keep pushing the boundaries. That's the only way we'll keep winning. We're nowhere near perfection. Only okay temperature control, but the balance in the sauces were off a little this time. Good but not great. Maybe we need to go to daily barbeque practice.

James rubbed his chin. If they cut back on some of their tactical training, maybe a bounty or two, they could get in more barbeque practice.

He grunted and chuckled. They were bounty hunters first and pitmasters second. He needed to keep that in mind.

Maybe in a few years, we can all retire and just focus on barbeque. That might not be such a boring life.

Shorty strutted back and forth with a huge smile on his face. "I know we're gonna take first this time. I'm telling y'all, that's how it's gonna happen. We represented just a month ago, and now we're gonna show all these bitches who the real power in barbeque is in California." He slammed his fist into his palm. "I don't even know why the rest of them bothered to show up. They just want to go back and cry to their mamas about how they got their asses handed to them by PFW, the Kings of Barbecue."

Max pulled off his glasses to wipe some grease off his face before putting them back on. "I'm feeling good myself. A lot of people were coming back for more food, and they were saying nice things about it. Not one person had anything bad to say."

James looked up from his phone. "Don't get too cocky. We've got tougher competition this time—a lot tougher. Did you guys taste any of the other teams' food?"

"Why bother with crap when you've got the prime shit right here? Don't want to ruin my refined sense of taste."

Several of them shouted their agreement.

James liked their enthusiasm, but he was worried they were building themselves up for disappointment. He'd sampled most of the other teams' food, and there were some quality efforts. The PFW saucing wasn't up to the same level as their efforts at Del Mar. He honestly wasn't sure they'd be able to win. It all depended on the judges now.

"Just saying you should be prepared in case we don't win. Even good barbeque can get passed over, depending on the day. It's like I've been telling you—mastering barbeque is harder than bounty hunting."

Shorty shrugged. "Come on, big man, don't be like that. It's just like with the bounties. We started with level ones and worked our way up to crazy-ass witches. We already had our training at Del Mar, and now we're ready to show that we're on the next level."

Trey snorted. He was sitting in a chair with his arms crossed, one of the few on the team who was not convinced they were going to win. For whatever reason, the man's cockiness extended into all areas of his life except his belief in the team's mastery of barbeque.

Good. Some things in life are sacred and shouldn't be taken lightly: Family, God, and barbeque.

Trey shook his head. "We ain't even have Mack here today. We're lucky if we place at all. Sauce was just…not there. Not shit, but not the best, either."

James raised an eyebrow, impressed by his protégé's improving palate.

Shorty picked up a rib and held it above his head like a sword. "Our sauce was damned fine. I respect Sergeant Mack as a cop and a pitmaster, but that ain't mean I'm not gonna do better than him. Students become the master and all that shit. That's how this is supposed to work. You know what I'm saying?"

James chuckled. It'd been almost a month since the museum incident, and since then neither he nor Shay had been in any serious trouble. The Brownstone Agency had been taking down bounties regularly in both Las Vegas and LA. A few annoying level threes had popped up in the previous week, but with a little off-the-books help from Tyler, James was able to surprise and capture them before they caused any serious trouble. It'd been quiet, at least by his standards.

The bounty hunter's gaze dipped to his shirt, where his amulet lay hidden. He'd bonded with it the previous week to finish off the level threes, just to be safe, but otherwise hadn't had much use for it. The power he'd tapped into during the museum incident had proven that Shay had been right and he'd not been using Whispy Doom to anywhere near maximum capacity, but the price for more power seemed to be lack of control. A weapon he couldn't reliably control was dangerous. Worse than that, it was complicated.

I have to be careful with this shit, so I don't hurt anyone I care about. The damned amulet seems to like me killing people, but he hasn't tried to get me to go after Shay, the cops, or any of my men, so at least he's got a fucking clue about which side he's on.

James shook his head and returned to looking at barbeque recipes. He didn't need armor or spikes to cook delicious brisket or ribs. He grunted, still pissed at people rating obviously shitty recipes so highly. Maybe it was a bunch of Oriceran who liked different flavor profiles.

He might as well stick to barbeque. From what Tyler and Lieutenant Hall had told him, all the big bounties were avoiding LA because they were afraid the Scourge of Harriken would rip their heads off.

Looks like I'm just going to have some time to relax. Maybe I can even get Shay to not go on so many tomb raids. After all our shit these last few months, we should take a nice little vacation together.

2

Crazak folded his hands in front of him as his fellow Council members all settled into their seats around the table, with the exception of He Who Hunts. The creature floated above his chair, glowing red eyes peeking out of his robe and a hint of the red mist inside showing below his sleeves. Although Crazak strove to avoid showing it, the murderous entity unnerved even the ruthless elf.

That one will be a problem sooner rather than later. It's unfortunate that he isn't more stable, but he'll be a useful tool for now. I suppose it was inevitable that these efforts would require such a diverse group and we'd have management difficulties at times, but we've made good use of these years.

He looked around the table. All had their hoods down except He Who Hunts. There was Lawrence, a wizard who had been Crazak's first recruit for the Council. Their gnome, Ferrao, had been the second. Yilin, an Eastern Frostling, had been the third.

The blue-skinned Yilin looked at him with her solid-black eyes. A frowning and deceptively young-looking witch, Elizabeth had been the penultimate recruit, and she'd recommended He Who Hunts, having dealt with him during certain ill-defined dark rituals.

Even now, Crazak wasn't sure if their final member was some sort of disembodied spirit or something else entirely. It didn't matter. His power was useful as a tool, and after what had happened with the museum artifacts, they needed all the power they could muster.

The elf cleared his throat. "I'll be the first to admit the last operation didn't go as smoothly as we would have liked. We all understand that. We lost all the artifacts we were going to use to raise further capital and garner influence, but we were able to preserve some of the more powerful ones for reproduction and to support our future operations. I'm still pleased with how things progressed, and all the loose ends have already been handled."

Yilin frowned. "You say that, but can anyone deny that this was a tremendous setback?"

Ferrao nodded his agreement. "A disaster. We spent months planning that operation. A partial success almost doesn't seem worth it."

Crazak shrugged. "It doesn't matter. Those responsible for the failure are all dead. We must simply accept that Los Angeles was a poor choice as a target city given some of the defensive resources there. We tempted fate, and she bit us. Lesson learned, but we accomplished our primary objective. For the artifacts we *did* recover, a small amount of research will allow us to mass-produce weaker versions. Once our operatives have access to that sort of thing, it'll ensure that embarrassments like Los Angeles won't happen again, even if certain parties choose to involve themselves in our business."

Lawrence drummed his fingers on the table. "Then we're going to proceed with the plan?"

The other elf nodded. "Yes. After all, our resources and influence continue to grow. The forces that would oppose us are looking for the wrong thing. They don't understand us, which means we have an advantage. They're looking for some dangerous conspiracy to control this sad little planet, not a group of wise beings who simply seek additional influence." He laughed. "After all, who cares about something so quaint as world conquest? We're not fools like Rhazdon."

Everyone at the table laughed except He Who Hunts. He didn't laugh unless it involved death.

Crazak's laugh faded to a simple chuckle. "We still have enough capital and artifact resources to continue with our next three objectives. As previously discussed, I will take responsibility for the first project. Yilin will handle the second project, and Ferrao will handle the third. We should begin to discuss the finer details of the—"

A flashing red orb winked into existence above the table.

Crazak frowned. He flicked his wrist, and a shimmering, floating image of soldiers, witches, and wizards stepping into the compound via a hole in the fence appeared above the table.

"It seems we've lost the advantage in this situation. Our assets here can at least clean this up." He rose, and another quick flick of the wrist summoned a swirling portal. "Meet at location three at the appointed time."

The others all created portals. The elf hesitated for a moment and looked over his shoulder.

No. All the others *hadn't* created portals. He Who Hunts glided toward the door.

I suppose he should be able to have some fun.

Crazak snickered and stepped through his portal.

"This is Hammer 1. All soldiers and agents have cleared the fence. No contact. Additional teams should launch. By the time the reinforcements get here, we'll have these guys nice and distracted."

"This is Salt 1. Roger that. Iron and Cold teams en route, ETA five minutes."

The two teams spread out in loose wedge formations, their weapons up.

Major Davies frowned. He'd expected at least a sentry by now, or some weird mechanical owl.

Didn't expect anyone to trace you here, did you? Wait, we've seen shit in the satellite photos. We know you don't keep this place that clean, so where the fuck are you hiding, you sons of bitches?

"Contact—" Sergeant Jeffries began to shout.

"Hammer 3, repeat." Major Davies spun toward the soldier. His exoskeleton lay on the ground, the soldier still strapped in with his head lolled back. Blood dripped from a gaping wound in his chest, where his armor had been shredded like paper.

"Hammer 3 down. Enemy contact," shouted Major Davies. "Does anyone have a target?"

One of the wizards muttered a quick spell, and a wave of light blasted from his wand and highlighted dozens of four-armed monsters. One stood right next to Sergeant Jeffries, towering over his body and licking its claws. An anti-magic deflector didn't do anything to protect a man from normal physical forces, if one could call claw wounds from a four-armed monster normal.

"Open fire," Major Davies ordered. "*Open fire.*"

The soldiers pulled their triggers, and anti-magic bullets blew chunks out of the monsters. With a screech, they charged the soldiers and agents.

A lightning bolt blasted from the roof of a nearby building and struck one of the witches. Her charred body flew several yards.

Heart pounding, Major Davies spun toward the source and saw a man covered with glowing glyphs on the roof. The soldier switched to burst fire and sprayed bullets toward the enemy wizard, but the arrogant bastard didn't even bother to dodge. He screamed as bullets tore through him and fell off the roof.

Didn't expect us to have anti-magic bullets, did you, asshole?

More of the four-armed monsters poured out several nearby buildings. A soldier near the major brought up his railgun. The weapon roared and made large holes through several of the monsters.

A claw tore out the throat of the wizard who'd killed the invisibility spell earlier. Two soldiers avenged his death by putting a few quick rounds into the monster's head, but that didn't do much to change the tactical situation.

A PDA witch swung her wand in a wide arc, and massive wave of green energy blasted the approaching monsters, their burn-covered forms squealing to the ground.

A massive fireball exploded against an invisible dome summoned by the team's surviving wizard.

"Roof at seven o'clock," Davies shouted.

Three soldiers fired in near unison, and the enemy wizard jerked almost like he was doing a little dance before he collapsed.

Squeals and inhuman screams echoed through the night as the soldiers put bullet after bullet into the charging monsters. The surviving soldiers started thinning the ranks of the enemies with the help of the surviving railgunners and grenades. The seconds stretched into eternity until finally no more monsters remained standing.

The surviving soldiers, along with the single wizard and witch left, searched the roofs and ground for more enemies.

Major Davis gritted his teeth and surveyed the carnage. The piles of dead monsters proved his men had given worse than they'd gotten, but Jeffries wasn't the only man who'd gone down.

"This is Hammer 1. Eagle 1, confirm vitals."

"This is Eagle 1. Hammer 1, we show only Hammer 1 and 2 with active vitals. Salt 2 and 3 are down, but Salt 5 and 6 are fine. Reinforcement ETA is three minutes."

"Everyone consolidate on my position," Major Davies ordered.

He reloaded his rifle and took stock of his resources. Salt 5 was a wizard, Salt 6 a witch, so they had defensive magic other than the deflectors. Hammer 2 had a railgun, and Salt 4 and 5 had rifles. Given their magic, deflectors, and anti-magic bullets, they could still take on a decent number of enemies. If the enemy had a reserve force, it had to be smaller than the horde they'd just thrown at them.

The major frowned. Or maybe the monsters were just a stall.

"Everyone reload. We're going to breach the building."

A second later a nearby door blew off its hinges, displaying a glowing hole in the center, and a cloaked form stepped from the building. No, stepped wasn't the right word. More like it glided, maybe even floated, though its robe extended to the ground.

Major Davies whipped up his gun and fired, and the cloaked figure jerked backward with a hiss. Another soldier fired off a grenade. It exploded over the target, shredding the cloak. The new holes revealed not a body, but a dense and thick red mist.

The new enemy charged straight toward Hammer 2, now openly flying through the air. The soldier raised his weapon and fired, but the cloaked monster jerked to the side, the round missing him and blowing a huge chunk out of a nearby wall.

What the hell? How does anything dodge a shot like that?

A red-mist tentacle whipped out of its sleeve and wrapped around Hammer 2's neck. He got out a scream before his entire head melted like ice under a heat lamp.

The surviving soldiers concentrated their fire. Their enemy jerked back several times, splattering glowing green ichor on the ground. The bastard cackled.

Keep laughing, asshole, but you're not escaping.

The witch attacked the cloaked menace with another green wave. The wizard lifted his wand, and with a flourish created a rippling shield between the team and their new enemy. Fortunately, the shield seemed to be one-way since Major Davies nailed their enemy with a few more shots.

The cloaked monster rose into the sky. Flying or jumping, it was hard to tell. It stopped at the edge of a nearby roof, leaving a glowing trail of ichor. Several orbs appeared in front of it, which shot out and pelted the shield.

The roaring of engines signaled the arrival of their reinforcements.

We've got you now, you sonofabitch.

VTOL insertion craft closed on the compound, their engines tilted at an angle. The engine shifted completely up, and they hovered over the site for a few seconds before descending.

The cloaked figure floated backward, a whirling gateway appearing behind him.

"Damn it," Major Davies muttered as their enemy drifted through the magical portal, which closed behind him.

He sighed. They'd lost men, but they'd killed several terrorists, and they still had their base to comb for intelligence.

I'm going to find you, you cloaked bastard, and finish you.

The insertion craft touched down near the surviving team members. The doors flew open and additional soldiers hopped off, this group lacking exoskeletons.

"Yeah," Major Davies began, "the bastards knew they couldn't wi—"

Several massive explosions ripped across the compound. The first few blew the landing craft apart and scattered the reinforcements. The next one knocked Major Davies to the ground.

I'm sorry, Emily. I hope your mom goes all-out for your first since I won't be there.

A final titanic explosion consumed him.

3

Captain Tanaka frowned, arms crossed, as he stared at the conflagration still consuming the remains of the compound. Firefighters choked the area, doing their best to contain the flames and prevent them from entering the forest. He wasn't so sure they'd win that fight.

Red and blue lights flashed all around him. An entire army of police was there, in addition to the National Guard troops they'd brought in to help secure the area. Now that this situation was no longer a quiet nighttime raid, they needed to be a little more careful about their use of military assets on American soil. As it was, there were more than a few questions about the whole incident that had only awkward answers.

Captain Tanaka turned to a nearby police officer. "And you're sure? The entire perimeter's been swept? Maybe someone was blown clear and survived?"

The officer shook his head. "They've found no one. I'm sorry, Captain, but everyone in your unit who went in there was wiped out. Nothing could have survived that fire, even with the help of magic."

Captain Tanaka gave a quick nod. He'd been monitoring the situation as Eagle 1 and was well aware that the two teams' vitals had stopped transmitting, but he'd held onto some small hope that some of the men and women had managed to survive the enemy's final desperate attack.

The police officer nodded to the captain and jogged toward a forensics team struggling to pull heavy equipment off their truck.

"You're going to have to think way out of the box when dealing with this group, Captain," remarked a voice behind Tanaka. "I've been saying that from the beginning."

Easy for you to say, elf.

Captain Tanaka shook his head, still looking straight ahead at the fire and not at the elf standing behind him. A lot of good soldiers had died in that raid, soldiers he'd known for years. He didn't need bland corporate slogans. He needed actionable intelligence.

"I've been examining the headcam footage. If the soldiers hadn't been surprised by the invisibility spell, they would have done better. The anti-magic bullets were working. If we'd just brought in air support from the beginning—"

"It would have been blasted out of the sky," interrupted the elf. "And keep in mind that your enemies weren't even using all the resources available to them." He sighed. "I've done my part. I've relayed what I've been able to figure out to your superiors, but the rest is up to you."

The captain continued staring at the flames, which were licking at a nearby tree almost like they were alive and ravenous. "Speaking of using all the resources available to us, if this group is as bad as you've said it is, doesn't it make sense that we should be bringing all our resources to bear rather than holding some back?"

"What do you mean?" A hint of suspicion colored the elf's voice.

Captain Tanaka frowned. "*Her*. You think she'll come back? Don't think I wasn't fully briefed on her. Impressive stuff. She's got a lot of experience dealing with dark magic."

The elf scoffed. "She's out of this game. Eventually, she'll come back, but don't try to push her. She did her time, and you know it. You humans need to find your next set of heroes. We have been trying to help you do this for decades."

The soldier shrugged. "Had to ask." He turned around to face the elf. "But I need something better to go off, Correk, than just, 'Think outside the box.' Berens might have done her time, but I just lost good friends. These Council bastards are obviously a serious danger to the United States, if not the world."

The elf shrugged and raised his hand, and a portal winked into existence. "I have a suggestion, then. Place a very large bounty on this group, dead or alive, a level six. I'm sure you'll find the expenditure of money worthwhile, and you'll find plenty of bounty hunters who know how to think outside the box."

Correk stepped through the portal, and it shrank to a dot before disappearing.

Captain Tanaka grabbed a passing soldier. "Sergeant, get me a damned phone."

Shay blinked at James from across the table. "I'm still annoyed that they're calling me 'Parkour Penny.' That name doesn't sound badass."

She held up his phone, which was playing a video of her doing a parkour run in downtown LA.

James grunted and shrugged. "Yeah, it's all over the net. I've been having them cleaned, just in case someone you've run into catches wind of it. I know we took down the cartel, and you took down that ice witch, but it's not exactly like you haven't made plenty of enemies."

Shay shrugged. "What can I say? I'm a people person." She chuckled at the phone. "I didn't realize I was getting caught so well on some of these videos. They should see what Lily and some of her friends can do. Makes me look like a total amateur. She's the real Parkour Penny."

She leaned forward, peering closer at James' phone. In the video, she jumped off the top of a building, caught a flagpole, and spun around it several times before letting go and flying to the top of the next building over.

The tomb raider grinned. "Damn. That was one a hell of a move right there. Totally badass. Even Lily couldn't do better than that, psychic reflexes or not."

James chuckled. "You should go on one of those ninja obstacle shows. You could win some easy money."

Shay shook her head and waved a hand. "Please. Bunch of pansies on those shows. If they want to make it good, they should force the contestants to do all those events with explosions or spells going off around you. At least a couple of crocodiles in the water if they fall in." She winked. "You should see what the latest Japanese version does. They take no prisoners there. They have a clause when you sign up where the contestant is damned near promised broken bones if they fall."

Explosions and spells, huh? Maybe I shouldn't be obsessing over better barbeque for my guys. Shay's got a point. The guys' training isn't always realistic.

James leaned back with a frown. "Damn."

"What's wrong?"

He shrugged. "My guys. It's just what you were saying. No crocodiles or explosions."

Shay blinked. "Huh? There aren't a lot of crocodiles in LA."

James shook her head. "I meant all the training for my agency. They do the tactical room training, and the obstacle courses, but maybe it's not good enough." He slapped his chest. "They're not me. They can't take the kind of pain and injury I can even without Whispy Doom. The more I train them up, the better and safer they'll be when they take on serious bad guys."

Shay nodded. "Couldn't hurt. Though it's not even like my setup at Warehouse One is filled with crocodiles." She frowned. "Though I don't have much in the way of mud, water, or pads. If I fall during training, I'm going to break something. It keeps me concentrating, and it's not like when I'm on a raid I can set up a bunch of safety equipment everywhere."

She selected another Parkour Penny video. This time, someone was trying to follow her, but they couldn't quite match her speed. James couldn't help but notice the cameraman kept focusing on her ass.

Fucker. Stay away from Shay's ass. That's mine.

James frowned at the video and grunted. He looked back up and tried to think of how he could improve the training at Camp Brownstone. Obviously, he didn't want to cripple his men or feed them to crocodiles, but maybe making things rougher wouldn't be such a bad idea. They weren't pussies. They could take it.

"Are you thinking what I'm thinking?" he asked.

Shay titled her head and grinned at him. "If it involves steaming up the shower without hot water, then yes."

"We'll have to put that on hold for a moment. What I was actually—"

His phone rang, interrupting the video. He frowned when he saw the caller ID.

Shit. Did something happen?

Maria sighed and took a sip of her drink. She looked up at Tyler, who was behind the bar, and shook her head.

He furrowed his brow. "What?"

"Too quiet."

Tyler glanced around the Black Sun. It was an unusually sparse crowd, but he didn't mind. Sometimes it was nice not to be filled to the brim with customers. Kathy was out this evening anyway so it would have been annoying to try to deal with everyone by himself.

He shrugged. "Nothing wrong with things being a little more sedate. Can't always have a crazy museum robbery or Drow queen attacking L.A., right?"

Maria shrugged. "I almost wish we did."

"Huh?"

She gulped down some of her drink. "Don't have anything to do with my team. Training's good, but actual action is better. Shit, there have barely even been any level threes we could go after, thanks to Brownstone and his men, and the SWAT team's not going to let us horn in on the level twos and lower." She groaned. "Don't get me wrong. It's not that I want some asshole to show up and hurt people, but it hasn't even been a month since we took on those assholes, and the brass is already bitching at me about budget, complaining that some of our money should be reallocated to different divisions." She slammed a fist on the bar. "It's like those assholes don't get that it's better to be prepared than apologize after the fact."

Tyler smiled. "You said yourself what the problem is."

"I did?"

He nodded. "Brownstone. And now not just Brownstone, but his whole Brownstone Agency thing. As long as he's in town, a lot of the high-profile scum aren't going to want to risk a visit. Maybe you should ask him to move to Vegas so a few of the bad guys start crawling back in."

Maria snorted. "Don't tempt me."

Tyler smirked. "With that last beatdown the AET and Brownstone delivered, the word on the street is LA is more trouble than it's worth unless you're willing to keep a low profile. Fuck, even the gangs and Mafia are laying low, worried that they might get Brownstone's attention and he'll go all Scourge of Harriken on their asses." His smirk disappeared. "And you know what happens to an information broker's business when all the criminals start dialing back on crime?"

The cop laughed and patted his hand. "Sorry to hear it."

"I don't know. Need to figure out something. Some way to make money."

She shot a glare at him. "If you dare arrange another pay-per-view fight, I swear I'll blow your balls off with a railgun."

Tyler rolled his eyes. "Give me a little credit. I'm a man of infinite flexibility. That's why my bar and business have flourished despite the many challenges to my business model."

"I thought it was more about just making the right bets. Sounds like you were lucky."

"Luck is where opportunity meets preparation, Maria." Tyler rubbed his chin. "Maybe I could pay Brownstone to stop by, put on a show, not a real bounty, just say Brownstone shit. Give the thrill-seekers a woody. Could do another Brownstone groupie event."

Maria laughed. "You think he'd agree to that?"

"If I cut him in and promise not to record it, maybe. The man respects making money, I'll give him that. Or I could just lie to him about some bounty."

"You want to risk lying to James Brownstone?"

Tyler sighed. "Good point. Now, what if we did a pay-per-view event that wasn't so dangerous?"

The cop groaned. "Are you fucking kidding me?"

"No, hear me out. You know, like we line up a bunch of level twos, like fifty of 'em. Battle royale against Brownstone. That kind of thing. No weird-ass fireball-slinging mages or Dark Elf queens, just your basic thugs." Tyler shrugged.

Maria took a deep breath and narrowed her eyes. "Have you ever seen what a railgun does to a wall?"

The information broker snapped. "Fine. Fuck the criminals. I've got a better idea. Same thing, battle royale, but with MMA fighters. We can tell Brownstone to hold back so he doesn't seriously hurt anyone, but I'm sure we can get some lawyer to make them all sign some contract where they acknowledge a serious risk of injury when taking on Brownstone."

"That is better than some dumbass Brownstone pay-per-view bounty hunt plan, but I doubt you could get a bunch of guys to agree to fight him after all the media coverage he's gotten. A fighter would have to be brain-dead to think they could win against him."

Tyler nodded a few times. "Yeah, you're probably right. Paparazzi photos? Candid Brownstone?"

Maria scoffed. "This is the same man who has EMPed police drones that were following and annoying him."

"That's why the good Lord invented the telephoto lens."

Maria took another sip of her drink. "And you think a tabloid's going to care about pictures of Brownstone at some sort of barbeque joint or something? Come on, you've hung around the guy enough and I've hung around Shay enough to know that he's not banging some groupie on the side. He gives money to an orphanage, and he fought hard to adopt a girl he didn't need to adopt."

Tyler scoffed. "You make the guy sound like the Pope. Look, I like Brownstone okay, but he's a pretty violent guy."

"Just saying, don't think the tabloids are interested in

him. His reputation isn't exactly a secret. It's not newsworthy."

"There's got to be an angle I'm missing." Tyler sucked in a breath and licked his lips. "Brownstone motivation videos. Oh, shit, Brownstone fight-training videos. We can make a whole series. I'll produce them and take a cut that way. It's totally legal."

Maria finished off her drink and set her glass down. "You really think Brownstone's going to go for that?"

"Maybe not anytime soon, but he's probably getting as bored as you are. He'll want something sooner than later. Should think of some other ideas." Tyler snapped. "Brownstone documentary. We'll call it *Granite Ghost: Scourge of Harriken.* We follow him all *cinema verité* style, like just a couple of weeks in the life of Brownstone. Maybe wait until things get a little hotter."

Maria shivered and gritted her teeth.

Tyler frowned. "Something wrong?"

"Yeah. You've always been on the wrong side of law and often on the wrong side of morality, but I never thought you'd sink so low as to consider joining Hollywood." Maria grinned and winked.

James slapped his phone to his ear. "Alison, are you all right?"

"I-I, um… Huh? Why do you sound so worried?" The girl on the other end sounded confused.

"It's pretty late here, so it's even later over there. If you're calling me in the middle of the night, I figure there's got to be something bad going on. You just give the word, and we'll hop a flight. Just tell me what kind of weapons we need to bring."

Shay frowned deeply. James switched the phone to speaker mode and set in on the table.

Alison sighed. "Nothing's bad, Dad. Nothing like that, anyway. I just, you know, wanted your advice. Maybe Aunt Shay's. It doesn't involve killing or shooting anyone."

"I'm here," Shay noted.

"Oh, good."

Wait. What kind of thing would Alison need advice from both Shay and me on...Oh, shit.

James grunted. "If this involves boys, I think you should wait. Five years."

Shay kicked him in the shin, and he shrugged.

Alison laughed. "I'm not exactly a little girl, you know. You want me to wait until I can drink before I date anyone?"

Shit, shit, shit. This is even worse than the Drow.

James scrubbed a hand down his face. "So it *does* involve a boy?"

"I'm just saying there's someone I like, okay? I've been thinking a lot about this, and I figure after everything that happened this summer, I kind of wanted to be more honest with you. So I figured if I told you in advance and if it turns into anything, then you won't come storming over here and blowing up half the school with some patented Dad rage."

"I've never blown up a school in my life," James muttered. "Well, I did blow up a classroom at a tech school once, but the bounty I was going after—"

"What your father means to say is that he understands you're an independent young woman," interrupted Shay, "and he wants to support your transition to adulthood by encouraging your responsible choices rather than being obnoxious and overbearing."

James sighed and rubbed the back of his neck. "I guess if I trust you enough to bring you along on bounties and have you fight witches, I can trust you around a boy, but if he does anything to upset you, I'm not promising I won't come over and have a loud one-way conversation with him. It may involve me kicking through a wall or two."

Alison laughed. "Okay, Dad, fair enough. Thanks. That makes me feel better. I was having some trouble sleeping, thinking that you'd come flying over here and tear up half the school once I told you."

"It's fine. Get some sleep."

"I will. Thanks. Thank you, Dad, and I love you."

"I love you, too," James replied.

Alison hung up.

Shay arched a brow.

James shrugged. "What?"

"Just, you're being mighty mature about this. I was half-expecting you to already be on the phone for a supersonic flight to Virginia."

He gave her a feral grin. "Nope. You're right. I need to let Alison grow up a little. So this guy gets one chance, but if she ever calls me up crying because of this boy I'm paying that school a little visit." He slapped a hand to his forehead. "Fuck."

Shay blinked. "What?"

"I forgot to get his name. You think she'll mind if I call her back to ask?"

His girlfriend just stared at him.

"Okay, okay, I won't call her back."

Yet.

4

General Francis nodded as he looked around the closed-door task force meeting. "DoD's already got this lined up with Homeland Security Three PDA teams. With the current plan, we've got two bounty hunter teams in the deal, and a third Special Forces team. The bounty hunters will be the bait for the bad guys, and our Special Forces boys will clean up while the bad guys are distracted. We've already got actionable intelligence on the location of several of the leaders of the so-called Council. Sound good to you?"

The other Joint Chiefs nodded their heads, and several other officials nodded as well.

"Did we watch the same footage?" asked Senator Johnston. He reached up to pull off his glasses and rub his eyes. "Two Special Forces teams, along with PDA support, got their asses handed to them. I don't see how adding bounty hunters to the mix helps that. We're already having a hard time with the media asking why a group of Army Special

Forces was attacking a corporate retreat on American soil. This is threatening to spin out of control."

Several of the gathered officials murmured their agreement.

An elegant woman leaned forward, threading her fingers together and rubbing a gold ring with her thumb. "I have to agree with Senator Johnston. The committee is ready to release whatever emergency funds as needed, but I'm not persuaded that sending more men through the grinder is the best idea. Maybe we should take some time to gather further intelligence on this."

"I understand that you're worried about that, Senator Silvers, but this is the best option." General Francis shook his head and looked at some of the people gathered in the secure conference room, including the Deputy National Security Advisor and a few other members of the task force. "We shouldn't wait on this. The longer we wait, the staler our intel becomes, and this group is magical. We have no guarantees they won't cast some spell tomorrow that'll let them sniff out our sources and take them out."

Senator Johnston frowned. "And what about my suggestion? I thought we were here to discuss alternatives."

"I'll take that into consideration, but the other resources are already all but in place." The general frowned. "This is an unusual threat, and we can't spend a lot of time pussyfooting around. Yes, we lost men, but the Council also lost people." He shrugged. "I invited you here today in a purely advisory capacity. We don't need additional Senate funding to proceed with this operation, and I *do* plan to proceed."

The senators exchanged glances.

The Deputy National Security Advisor shrugged. "The National Security Advisor has made it clear that the President is deferring to us on this matter, although he's more concerned with results than details."

Senator Johnston shook his head. "You mean he wants to be firewalled away from any fuck ups."

"If we don't fuck up, we won't have a problem. I think the plan presented makes the most sense, and I *don't* think we have time to sit around debating everything."

The two senators frowned but said nothing.

General Francis stood. "I agree. It's time to set the plan in motion. We've got good intelligence on the targets. I think we can have boots on the ground within twenty-four hours. It's a shame we lost good soldiers before, but they'll be avenged soon enough."

The Deputy National Security Advisor nodded. "Let's finish off these assholes ASAP. If they're dead, it doesn't matter what questions the media asks. We'll meet again after the completion of the operation."

The various officials began to stand and file out. Senator Silvers followed Senator Johnston into the hallway, her lips pursed.

She shook her head. "Be honest, what do you think is going to happen?"

Senator Johnston grunted and sighed. "We're going to lose a lot of good people on this clusterfuck, and in the end, we're going to do it the way I would have suggested."

"Which is what, exactly? You mentioned something, but I didn't hear any details in the meeting." Senator Silvers shrugged.

"I'd already talked to the general about it. He was

supposed to bring it up at this meeting." Senator Johnston locked eyes with her. "When you want a pit of vipers taken out, you find the man or woman with the biggest fucking boots to do the stomping. You don't send a bunch of people to half-ass it. And right now, no one has bigger boots than James Brownstone. He has tangled with them before, so it only makes sense to send him again."

He started down the hallway, and the other senator matched his pace.

"Well, the general *did* mention bounty hunter teams," Senator Silvers commented. "Maybe Brownstone will be on one of those."

Senator Johnston shrugged. "Did you look at the personnel notes? They are claiming it was open, but they've already handpicked their teams. Brownstone isn't anywhere near this operation."

"Probably a good idea anyway. I find it hard to believe that he'd want to help the government after everything that happened with his daughter. The last thing we need is a loose cannon involved in such a sensitive matter."

Senator Johnston chuckled. "The government's a big organization, and I'm pretty sure Mr. Brownstone understands that not everyone in it has it out for him. The problem with most people is they see a man with muscles on his muscles, a man who uses his fists to punctuate his sentences, and they assume he's stupid. There's a lot going on in that head of his, and he shouldn't be underestimated."

The woman offered him a smile. "If you say so."

They lapsed into silence and continued walking.

Senator Silvers kept the frown off her face, even though she was worried. She'd hoped she could steer the government away from interfering with her masters, especially after the fiasco with the first raid, but now they were doubling down on their efforts.

And Brownstone. He might be trouble.

After a few more steps, she allowed herself a small smile. No. Brownstone might be powerful, but he was only one man, and he mostly confined himself to Los Angeles. He'd beaten low-level disposable garbage.

I saw you at your little contest in Del Mar, so smug and self-assured. You're nothing *before my masters. Maybe I should encourage Johnston's plan just to get you killed.*

Senator Silvers forced herself to stop smirking before Senator Johnston noticed.

James and Shay stepped into the Leanan Sídhe. Even more bodies than normal choked the pub, and everyone was cheering and whooping.

Whatever this is, it can't be good for me, James thought.

After a few steps, the bounty hunter grunted at the large banner hanging over the bar.

BARD OF FILTH COMPETITION.

The bounty hunter sighed, and Shay snickered.

"Damn it," James muttered. "I should have paid more attention to when it was happening next."

"It's Brownstone," someone shouted.

The crowd parted, clearing a path from James and Shay to the Professor. The older man stood in front of the banner, ruddy-faced and smirking. A disappointed frat boy next to him hung his head.

The Professor turned his grin on James. "The competition's over and I've defended my title, but how about a little exhibition round? A little something for the fine crowd."

James frowned. "What the fuck do you mean by that?"

I should have never come here tonight.

"You almost beat me once, lad, and even though you can't win the title from one limerick, your adoring public does await." The Professor threw his hands to his sides. "Do you want to hear him deliver some dirty limericks?"

The crowds cheered and started chanting, "Brown*stone*."

James scrubbed his face with his hand. "I did that shit before because I owed you, and I'm never doing it again. Get over it."

The chanting died down, with more than a few disappointed faces appearing in the crowd.

Fuck all of you.

Shay grinned. "What about me?"

The Professor raised an eyebrow and grabbed a mug of beer off the bar to take a drink. "That I'd almost pay to hear." He raised his mug above his head. "If James won't give us what we want, how about we let the lovely Miz Carson deliver us a quick limerick?"

The crowd roared their approval and started chanting, "Car*son*."

James sighed and shook his head, then leaned against the bar and crossed his arms. As long as he wasn't doing it, there was only so much he could complain.

The noise died down to a mere murmur. Shay furrowed her brow and stared down at the ground. When she lifted her head, she stared right at James with the largest shit-eating grin a human could achieve without magic.

The bounty hunter grimaced and resisted the urge to run for the door.

Oh fuck. This is gonna be bad. Drow-queen bad.

Shay cleared her throat and turned to the crowd.

"There once was a sailor named Jacques,

Toughest bastard near the docks,

At night, he did not kill,

Instead, he chose to spill,

Cum from his largest of cocks."

The Professor smirked. James groaned and face-palmed. The audience, in contrast, exploded in laughter and cheers.

James blinked.

At least it wasn't about me. But, shit, she pulled that out after just a few seconds of thinking? I had to get special training to pull it off.

"Car*son*, Car*son*, Car*son*!" the crowd chanted.

The Professor held up his hand, and the crowd quieted after a few more chants.

"Alas, Miz Carson, because you didn't participate in the full competition you can't win, but had you, you might now be the new Bard of Filth." Smite-Williams shook his head. "I'm glad you came too late."

Shay smirked and crossed her arms. "Maybe next time you have one of your little contests, I'll stop by to display my fine wordsmithing to your drunk ass."

He smiled. "Please do. I'll have to bring my A game next time, Miz Carson." He waved to the crowd. "But the competition and exhibition are over for now. Please enjoy the rest of your night."

The crowd began to break up, murmurs and chatting filling the pub.

The Professor nodded to a table across the room. James and Shay made their way over there while he took a few moments to shake people's hands and get a new mug of beer. When he finally dropped into a seat across from them, his face was redder than a lobster.

James grunted. "You're the one who called us, but you seem more like Father O'Banion than Professor Smite-Williams at the moment. How the fuck are we supposed to talk about business when you're like that?"

Shay snickered.

The older man waved a hand. "Even Father O'Banion can be professional when he needs to be." He punctuated the sentence by gulping down more beer. "And it's not much business. At least not yet. I just wanted to give you a little heads-up, lad, concerning the museum thieves."

James snorted. "What do I care? They're all dead."

He resisted growling. Those bastards had dared to kidnap Shay, and he was only irritated that he couldn't kill them again. He didn't give a shit if Whispy Doom liked it. The amulet's bloodlust and his desire to protect his woman had worked together nicely.

"That they are," the Professor replied, "but their employers aren't, and there are still several artifacts unaccounted for that their employers likely have their hands on."

"Employers? Those guys weren't the ones running it?"

Shay leaned forward. "Makes sense. That crew didn't

seem quite at the level to be coordinating all that shit themselves, and the level of magic they had was a bit much for some snatch-and-grab thieves."

The Professor nodded. "The government, with the aid of other interested parties, has determined that a group called 'the Council' is involved. They were able to locate a hideout and they launched a raid, but their forces were wiped out. Now they have a new plan based on some newer information. They're recruiting elite bounty hunters as part of two teams to go after them." He sighed and shook his head.

James shrugged. "What's the problem, then? If the government's putting together a bunch of badasses, they'll finish off these Council fuckers soon enough. I killed the guys I needed to kill already."

The Professor frowned. "Have they contacted you?"

The bounty hunter shook his head. "Nope."

"And you don't want in? These people, however, indirectly, did injure you and yours."

James shrugged. "The fuckers who were responsible for taking Shay and threatening Alison are dead, so I don't know if I really give a fuck. If they want me, they need to come and ask, especially since this shit doesn't sound like it's just a matter of driving to Lincoln Heights to kick some ass. I don't want to fly halfway across the world to do it."

The Professor picked up his mug and gulped the contents before slamming it down on the table. "I *want* you to go, lad. I'm concerned about some of those artifacts, and I'd feel better knowing you were involved. I also know you can resist certain dangerous temptations. I can't say that for every bounty hunter who might otherwise be involved."

Shay chuckled. "It's negotiation, Professor. First off, it's not like James is responsible for stopping every bad thing that happens in the world. If the government wants him involved, they can come with a truck full of money. And it's not like they didn't have a chance to contact him already. James isn't exactly an obscure figure in the world of bounty hunting." She shrugged. "Not only that, it's not like he has any reason to trust the government. Whenever they're involved someone's going to get screwed, so it'd be better if they came with hat in hand."

James grunted and nodded his agreement.

The Professor sighed. "I can see what you're saying, but I do want those items out of circulation. I'll have to ask around and see what their plan is. If we're lucky, the government's plan will go well even if you're not involved."

A waitress appeared with a new beer.

He smiled up at her. "Just in time. Don't want to risk sobering up."

James could see the disappointment on the Professor's face, but he didn't care. The Council wasn't his business until someone made it his business.

About an hour later, Shay pulled her Fiat into a parking spot in front of a liquor store.

James looked at her. "We were just at a bar. Why are we stopping here?"

"Because we didn't drink at the bar. We just watched Smite-Williams drink, and I want to make you a Three Wise Men. I think you'd like it." She shrugged. "Always trying to find new ways to force you outside the tiny box you call life. Tonight my method is triple whiskey."

He grunted and got out his earbuds. "Okay, I'm just going to listen to a little barbeque podcast while you're shopping then. No reason for me to go in there."

Shay smirked. "It's not like I'm going in there for a new fall wardrobe. It won't take that long."

James shrugged. "Now that I'm leading a barbeque team in competition, I need to live and breathe barbeque."

She laughed and opened the door. "If you lived and breathed barbeque any more than you do now, you'd start sweating God Sauce."

Shay shut the door and headed toward the liquor store, shaking her head. Her last glance over her shoulder at her man revealed that he was looking down, his eyes closed and his earbuds in.

He's changed a lot, but he's more fanatical than ever about barbeque. Don't know if that's a good thing or a bad thing. At least he doesn't hate pizza.

Shay chuckled a little and entered the store, an electronic chime signaling her entrance. The bored-looking clerk gave her a polite nod. She grabbed a basket and then headed toward the whiskey section. A little private booze party would make her night fun.

Let's see. They have plenty of Johnnie Walker, Jim Beam, and Jack Daniels. Wonder if I should grab some others as an experiment?

She reached down to grab a few bottles.

How much whiskey is too much?

The car screeched to a halt in the liquor store's parking lot, and the hoods pulled on their ski masks and grinned at each other.

"You ready?" asked one.

His partner nodded, and they looked at the driver. "Keep the fucking engine going so we don't have a repeat of that bullshit from last time. I still can't believe that shit."

The driver shrugged. "Not my fault the engine had trouble starting. I told you we needed to replace the solenoid."

"Just saying. Keep the engine going."

The first hood opened his door and pulled out his gun on his way to the entrance. The second hopped out and sauntered after him.

"Put your hands up, and nobody fucking move," the first hood shouted after he threw open the door.

The clerk raised his hands high, a weary look on his face but not much fear.

Two customers standing in line quickly set their booze on the counter and lifted their hands as well, their eyes wide.

The second hood moved from aisle to aisle, his gun out. The most annoying thing about robberies was when he ran into damned wanna-be heroes. He frowned as he spotted a hot dark-haired woman holding a basket filled with whiskey bottles.

Maybe she'd been listening to music and just didn't hear him, but he couldn't see any earbuds.

"What the fuck are you doing, bitch?"

Being hot didn't mean he was going to let her fuck up their robbery.

The woman looked at him. "What? You talking to me?"

There wasn't even a hint of fear on her face, even though he was the one with a gun.

The hood brandished his pistol. "This is a fucking robbery. Do you understand that, bitch?"

She shrugged. "Look, I'm trying to make some serious booze decisions here." She waved him away dismissively. "Just go away and leave me alone."

The hood stomped over to her. Now she was disrespecting him. He didn't need a murder rap, but maybe a few weeks in the hospital would teach the woman some respect. He swung his gun at her. A little pistol whipping would shut her mouth.

The dark-haired hottie jerked back, dodging his attack. He swung again, but she spun to the side, her bottles clinking in her basket.

His heart rate kicked up. He didn't understand how she was dodging him.

The woman glared at him. "Last chance, asshole."

"Stay still, you fucking whore," the man screamed, "or I'll fucking kill you. You understand me?"

She narrowed her eyes and set her basket down. "*What* did you just say to me?"

The man smirked. "Yeah, that's better. Get on your knees and say you're sorry. Maybe I won't beat your ass then for disrespecting me."

She cracked her knuckles. "I've got a different suggestion."

"What's that, bitch?"

Her knee was in his stomach before he'd even registered that she'd moved. He doubled over, his dinner threatening to come up. Lightning-fast punches pounded his face, and he was unconscious before he even hit the ground.

James looked down at his phone. If he'd been looking up, maybe he would have spotted the powerful roundhouse kick Shay delivered to the other thug. The man spun several times before slamming face-first into the ground. She leaned over and shook her finger at him, an angry scowl on her face.

"Now, what you need to do," explained the podcast host with a slow drawl, "is be willing to experiment. Sometimes it's not about new ingredients or spices, but just about how you combine what you have. A little more vinegar here, a little less molasses there. You can try a different pepper or two. Don't obsess over an exact recipe. That's how your barbeque becomes boring and stale."

James grunted. This was all solid advice. One thing that competing had made him realize was that for all his appreciation of the different types of barbeque, he wasn't adventurous enough when it came to preparing his own, which meant he wasn't a true lover of the ultimate form of cooking. A true pitmaster would be able to prepare delicious barbeque for different people with different tastes.

I need to do better. Maybe I should challenge the guys to experiment more. If they all do their own thing, we can all get better as a team.

His eyes flicked to the rearview mirror for a moment.

"Everyone wants to talk about Nadina," the podcaster

continued. "And, yeah, the fact that the little elf girl won shows there's a whole range of possibilities out there, but keep in mind that she stayed true to her roots, which is why I think she won. It wasn't that she was exotic, but rather the opposite if you think about it. She experimented with what she already knew."

James sighed. If only everything were about barbeque, the world would be a better place.

Shay waved to the clerk as she headed toward her car, her bottles in a bag. The police were on their way, and the clerk had comped her liquor in exchange for stopping the robbery.

She laughed when she saw James still staring down at his phone. She'd been kicking ass while he was listening to barbeque shit.

Her gaze cut to an empty car in the lot.

That must have been theirs. Better not mention anything about the robbery since he didn't notice. Don't want to ruin the mood.

Shay opened the driver-side door and slid inside. "Hear anything exciting?"

James looked up from his phone and shook his head. "Just normal stuff."

The bounty hunter pounded down his third mixed drink as he took in the sight of his woman in her negligee kneeling next to him on the bed. The Three Wise Men was a nice drink, but he preferred to get straight to the action rather than worrying about more whiskey.

Shay wrapped her arms around him and gave him a deep kiss before pulling away with a smirk. "I have to say, for such a badass you're not that observant."

James grunted. "I'm observant enough. I like what I see right now."

She shook her head. "Not what I'm talking about. There was a robbery at the store. Gave me a nice workout when I took the thugs down, but all the while you sat and listened to your podcast."

He grinned. "For a tomb raider, *you're* not very observant."

Shay frowned. "Huh?"

"You didn't even notice their driver."

She shook her head. "They didn't *have* a driver. I saw their car, but no one was in it."

"Yeah, because I knocked his ass out, and he was sprawled forward."

"Why didn't you say anything?"

He shrugged. "Didn't want to ruin the mood."

They stared at each for a few seconds before laughing.

Shay smiled. "Well, I guess I didn't complete my workout, because I missed the third guy. I'll need your help with making sure I have an...appropriate workout today."

James grunted. "Anytime, anyplace, and all night long, preferably."

5

Harrier slapped a magazine containing anti-magic bullets into his rifle. "Damn, I should have been working straight for the government this entire time. Giving us exact coordinates and flying our asses out there? That shit's a lot easier than what I've had to deal with for most bounties."

The hulking George chuckled as he inspected his machine gun. He pulled an anti-magic deflector out of a belt pouch and slipped it over his neck. "This your first level six?"

The other bounty hunter shook his head. "First state-side. Hit one in Mexico once. Had to dig the fucker out of the mountains."

"This is my first six, but I've hit tons of fives," commented Lise. The blonde bounty hunter pulled her hair into a ponytail before grabbing her helmet. Like the rest of her unique power armor, it was bright blue.

The only man without a gun was the short and ironically-named Big Tim. The wizard had no armor, and not much in the way of supplies other than a wand holster.

"Do we have much on the targets?" the wizard asked. "That briefing was kind of a joke, except the size of the reward."

Harrier shook his head. His heart had already sped up like it did before every job. He didn't believe in staying calm. Being freaked meant adrenaline, and that meant faster reactions. Keeping calm didn't mean shit as long as he was the one still breathing at the end of the fight.

"Nope, just that two of the Council are in the warehouse. They have offensive and defensive magic, along with summoning abilities. We should expect weaker magical support and monsters, and a few anti-magic bullets should be enough to deal with the monsters."

Lise slipped her helmet on and tapped a control on her wrist. "Nice to not have to take any prisoners. That'll make this easy." Her voice sounded hollow and distant through her helmet speaker.

"Let's do this shit already," George rumbled. "Nothing like getting rich. I think I'm gonna take a long vacation after this one."

Harrier shook his head. "We're waiting for the signal. Need to do this shit simultaneously." His watch beeped, and he laughed. "Okay, there we go. Speak of the Devil and then go kick his ass."

He grinned and threw open the back door of the truck. The four bounty hunters piled out of the vehicle. Their driver was long gone, at their insistence. They didn't want some government stooge getting in their way.

Even if they didn't normally work as a team, they all

knew each other's general capabilities and could avoid blowing someone up who didn't have it coming.

Big Tim raised his wand and performed several quick movements. Several dozen tiny glowing orbs appeared and swirled around the group in an erratic pattern.

They marched in a rough line toward the warehouse, and Harrier nodded to Lise. "Do it."

She tapped her wrist control. A distant whirring and buzzing grew louder and closer over several seconds until they could make out a dozen drones closing on the warehouse. The bounty hunters watched as the drones slammed into the roof of the warehouse and exploded. A cloud of debris rained from the sky as half the roof collapsed.

"Damn!" George shouted. He laughed and shook his head. "They *did* say dead or alive."

Several more explosions blew holes in the warehouse's first-floor walls. Men with guns and wands poured out, shooting and slinging fire and energy bolts. Tim's orbs stopped orbiting and flew toward the bullets and spells to absorb them with a flash.

George lifted his heavy machine gun and grinned. His barrel spat lead in a steady stream, blowing man after man apart. Harrier slung his rifle over his shoulder and pulled out his pistol. No reason to waste anti-magic bullets on the peons.

Lise raised her arms and fired several micro-rockets from the launchers on her armor. The explosives slammed into the defenders, blowing several of them to pieces and spreading even more fire over the already burning warehouse.

A blue-skinned woman stepped to the edge of the roof.

Harrier and Lise tried to shoot her, but their rounds bounced off a flashing blue shield and fell to the ground encased in ice.

A frowning gnome surrounded by a shimmering cloud joined her on the side and shook his head.

Harrier nodded to Lise. "Let Big Tim and George handle the defensive line." He holstered his pistol and grabbed his rifle. "Let's finish off the quarterbacks."

He knelt for a moment and muttered a quick phrase in Old Norse. Futhark runes appeared on his boots, and he leapt toward the roof.

Lise fired a grappling hook at the edge of the roof and caught it. Soon, both bounty hunters were heading straight for the Council members.

Just as they brought up their weapons to fire, an opaque sphere of ice froze around the targets.

"Damn it," Harrier muttered as he hit the roof. He grabbed a grenade and waited for Lise.

She rolled onto the roof and aimed one of her micro-rocket launchers at the ice shield.

The thunder of gunfire and exploding spells continued below, but Harrier kept his attention on the sphere.

"Three…two…one," he counted and tossed his grenade.

Lise launched another volley of rockets. Chunks of ice blasted away from the orb. Harrier could make out the shadowy outlines of the two Council members before all the ice was clear, and he and Lise opened fire.

The blue-skinned woman jerked a few times, red blood blossoming from her wounds. Lise whipped out a pistol and opened fire with exploding bullets.

Harrier grinned. They were winning, they just needed

to keep up the attack. A large piece of cement slammed into him and knocked him to his side. A follow-up explosion knocked him toward one of the holes in the ceiling. He grabbed the edge before falling and pulled himself up one-armed, not willing to lose his rifle.

"What the fuck?" He groaned, his body throbbing.

Lise's bullets kept changing direction at the last second.

Harrier gritted his teeth. He knew she was using anti-magic bullets, just like he was.

Razor-sharp ice tendrils condensed from the air and pierced Lise's armor in several places. She screamed, but the tendrils kept perforating her. She stumbled back, red blood painting her blue armor, and pressed a button on her wrist control

No rockets came out this time. Instead, a bright blast of glowing stones hit the blue-skinned woman and gnome.

A second later, a tendril stabbed the bounty hunter through the heart. Her helmeted head lolled forward, and she stopped moving.

Another piece of cement slammed into Harrier.

Where the fuck is that coming from?

He groaned and turned. Three smiling wizards floated off to the side of the building.

One of the wizards held George and Big Tim's heads, and he tossed them onto the roof with a smirk.

"Fuck you," Harrier yelled. He rolled and grabbed his gun, switching to full auto, and unloaded the rest of the anti-magic clip into the three wizards. The men tumbled to the ground in a shower of their own blood.

The gnome grinned from inside the remains of the ice

orb. He held what looked like a heavy-tipped lawn dart. "You've done well."

He nodded toward the blue-skin woman. She was on her knees, blood pouring from a dozen wounds, whereas the gnome had a single minor head wound.

The gnome made a gesture with his hand, and the dart disappeared. "I don't even need this. Don't feel too bad. There were only four of you, but you killed most of our people. That's an achievement." He sighed. "And an unfortunate loss of resources. Feel some pride before you die."

Throbbing agony distracted Harrier as he yanked another anti-magic magazine from his tactical harness. "You're dead, you son of a bitch. She's fucked up and bleeding, and you're wounded. You're not gods."

The bounty hunter tried to eject his magazine and load the new one, but his shaking and weak hands couldn't seem to pull off the motion, and his ammunition dropped to the roof with a clink.

The gnome shrugged. "And *you're* not even us. Think about that as you die." A whirling portal appeared, and the gnome dragged the blue-skinned woman through it with a frown.

Harrier clenched his jaw, trying to fight off the darkness that threatened to swallow him.

Fuck, I'm bleeding out. Need to get to my potion. I can... I can still do this.

The bounty hunter stopped breathing. His last sight was the gnome's hand waving to him before he disappeared into the portal.

We can do this. The Wu family has brought down plenty of level fives. Time to show the world we can take down level sixes, too.

Dozens of fearless bronze and iron statues holding heavy curved swords marched forward, ignoring the bullets and fireballs blasting around them. Scorch marks and chips indicated the hits, but the statues' expressions didn't change.

"Keep them going, May," Cheng Wu yelled to his daughter. He reloaded his enchanted repeating crossbow and fired into the monsters. His bolt exploded and scattered several of them.

The young woman kept both hands tightly on her wand as her warriors slammed into the line of four-armed monsters that had emerged from the mansion. Their claws scratched at her animated statues to little effect. She smiled as her creations brought down their mighty swords and cleaved the first group of monsters in half. They'd already finished off all the gunmen and wizards the Council members had brought with them.

You Council jerks don't know who you're dealing with.

Fire, lightning, and strange prismatic rays rained down on the flickering dome her two sisters maintained over the family.

They were so close. According to the information the government had given them, the elf, witch, and wizard standing behind the horde of monsters were their primary targets, members of the mysterious and dangerous Council.

Just need to hold off their monsters, and we can break through and take them out.

Her father's plan had worked. The defensive forces had

concentrated on his daughters and him, never expecting they had two more men with them—her brothers. Not only that, they each carried powerful magical swords.

Almost there. Almost there.

May smiled as she spotted Harry and Tony on the roof above the Council members. Without a word both dropped, pointing their swords down.

We win, Council.

Harry's blade slid through the witch's heart. Tony nailed the wizard's arm, but it wasn't an instant kill. The elf frowned and leapt back a dozen yards as if magically tossed by an invisible hand.

He whipped up his hand, and a complex series of glyphs appeared in the air. Two bright rays blasted from his hand and through Harry and Tim.

May blinked several times as her brothers fell to the ground, large holes in their chests.

"Keep up the attack," her father yelled, "or we're all dead."

The elf spun toward the rest of the family. May jerked her head toward her sisters and realized they'd dropped their wands in shock.

"Harmony, Lindsey!" she shouted. "*The dome*!"

Her father fired a bolt at the elf, which exploded but didn't muss a hair on the target's head. He growled and fired another bolt at the wounded wizard. The explosion knocked the man back and he dropped to the ground, charred and twitching.

The elf raised his hands. Two more rays blasted out, carving holes through May's father and Lindsey.

May trembled, her heart thundering. She made several

quick motions with her wand, and a half-dozen of her statue warriors broke away from the few remaining monsters and lumbered toward the elf.

They slashed at him, their blows striking an invisible shield around him. May kept up the attack. Once the last of the monsters fell to her other soldiers' blades, she sent the entire group. The elf blasted the heads off a couple, but they kept attacking.

That weakens them, but it's not enough, you bastard. You're going to pay for what you did to my family.

One of the statues' blades finally made it through the elf's shield and slashed his chest. He slapped his hands together, and a massive wave of energy knocked the statues to the ground. The hot wave slammed into May and Harmony.

Every cell in May's body felt like it was on fire. She hissed and blindly patted the ground around her to try to find her wand. Her fingers reached it just as a portal appeared in front of the elf, who limped through it, his arm outstretched and the wizard floating behind him.

May crawled over to Harmony. Her younger sister was unconscious and bleeding, but still breathing.

Her other sister, brothers, and father were all dead. May wiped tears from her eyes and glared at the dead witch's body.

6

Crazak hissed as he emerged from the portal, Lawrence in tow. Ferrao was pacing back and forth with a frown. Yilin knelt on the ground, ice covering several obvious wounds. He Who Hunts glided over the ground, a sinister specter in front of an otherwise nondescript but large rustic mountain cabin.

Dozens of wizards and armed men stood in lines, awaiting orders. It was fortunate the Council had planned for this eventuality, even if Crazak was still shocked at just how savage the government attacks had proven so far.

We overplayed our hand. Subtlety might have served our cause better for a few years.

"Where's Elizabeth?" Ferrao asked.

"Dead," Crazak muttered. "We underestimated those government fools." He shook his head. "Are the air defenses still active? If they knew to attack us at those other locations, they might know about this one."

A wizard stepped toward him and nodded. "Yes, sir. If

any government aircraft even gets close to this area, we'll be able to shoot them down with minimum effort."

Crazak nodded. "Fine. We can lick our wounds a little here. We're too far away for them to attack us without a massive number of portals or aircraft, so it'll be fine. We'll have to consider our next step. We might need to abandon our American locations temporarily and rebuild operational strength."

The ice melted on Yilin's wounds and several closed, but she wasn't completely healed. "I thought our contacts were supposed to assure these sorts of things didn't happen?"

He Who Hunts chuckled lightly. "Death comes for all eventually, regardless of power. Such is the way of existence."

Ferrao snorted. "And what of you?"

"Yes, even me eventually."

Crazak shook his head. "The past is irrelevant. We still have resources and forces we can muster—"

A massive explosion hundreds of feet up shook the area, and a few seconds later a missile exploded against the aerial defensive field.

Damn it! So soon?

"They know we're here." The elf clenched his jaw. "Everyone, prepare for an attack," he shouted. "We must make our enemies pay in blood for daring to oppose the Council."

Dozens of dark streaks filled the horizon. Seconds ticked past before the missiles smacked into the shield, producing grand explosion after explosion. The bombardment continued for a good half-minute, but toward the end Crazak chuckled, some of his tension flowing away.

Arrogant fools overplayed their hand.

"They think they can brute-force their way in?" He shook his head. "We can evacuate before they even know what's happenin—"

A loud roar preceded screams from guards and wizards as a railgun round tore through a half-dozen men. Dozens of uniformed men in exoskeletons rushed from the opposite side, the US Army.

What? How?

Crazak's eyes widened as more soldiers rushed through a portal, followed by several witches and wizards. He'd been so focused on the bombardment he hadn't even sensed the portal magic.

The soldiers quickly spread out, their rifles spewing anti-magic bullets and shredding the wizards and armed guards. Railgun rounds and grenades pelted the area, and less than thirty seconds after the soldiers had arrived they'd reduced half the support forces to red paste.

The Council troops' guns proved ineffective against the heavy armor of the advancing Special Forces, and their distracted wizards and witches took too long to start flinging elemental and magical death toward the arriving enemy. Counterspells in various forms—orb, field, and bolt—zoomed out to meet the Council wizards' magic.

The cacophony of the battle swallowed the *thunk* of several grenades being launched into the air. The soldiers continued moving forward, their mix of weapons tearing up the ground and cutting through the lesser magic users' defenses.

"It's time to leave," Crazak announced, throwing up a shimmering magical shield. "Our brave servants can slow our enemies' advances. I'll give them credit for their tactics, and we'll make them pay for it later."

Ferrao grimaced and snapped, "It won't open."

Crazak raised his hands to summon a new portal and frowned. *Nothing*. Something was blocking the spell.

Damn you.

He glared at the wizards and witches in the rearguard behind the soldiers. They had to be the source of the disruption. Once they died, the Council would be free.

Explosions ripped up the ground around the Council members and strained the shield. It flashed with each hit, and more than a few bullets slid through, albeit slowly, dropping to the ground shortly after entry.

How many anti-magic bullets do these damned soldiers have? At least they're putting a grand effort into trying to kill us.

The flash and loud report of gunfire ceased. Crazak surveyed the area. The soldiers were spreading around the Council members. All their servants and guards lay dead. The government's witches and wizards walked slowly forward but remained well behind the soldiers.

We will die here, but not to these mere servants.

All the enemies raised their weapons and opened fire. Ferrao and Crazak both gritted their teeth, feeding more energy into the shield. Yilin stood, unsteady on her feet. Lawrence groaned and sat up, one of his arms hanging limply.

"If we have no servants," Crazak shouted, "then we should summon new ones. Ferrao, hold the shield. The rest of us will do what is needed."

The gnome nodded and half-closed his eyes, both arms up.

Crazak raised his hand and muttered several incantations, and glowing glyphs appeared around a small swirling portal. Yilin raised her hands, and a bright blue ring surrounded the portal. Multiple streams of energy poured from He Who Hunts. A low groaning hum filled the area, building in volume over several long seconds as the portal swirled faster and faster. The elf flung his arms upward, and a bright flash blinded everyone for a few seconds.

The foolish witches and wizards helping the soldiers had anticipated blocking portals to another part of Earth or maybe even Oriceran, not somewhere far darker and more dangerous.

Dozens of jet-black holes opened in the sky above them. Looking into them was like staring directly into the abyss. Dark, shuddering monsters with hungry tentacles and tooth-filled maws started dropping from the holes.

To their credit, the soldiers took only moments to recover, the majority raising their weapons and opening fire on the new threat. Bullet after bullet ripped into the falling hungry monsters, some of the barrages blowing enough of the creatures apart that they sizzled and disappeared.

It wasn't enough. A shadow rain of ravenous, hideous monsters continued to pelt down. A demon rain.

Crazak chuckled. Now their enemy would die. A loud railgun round answered his arrogance, and it pierced their depleted shield. Even at reduced velocity, it removed the bulk of Lawrence's head.

The remaining Council members strengthened Crazak's shield. The next railgun round bounced off with a flash, but the dark portals above began to shrink and close one by one, a few slicing their arrivals in half. No mercy *from* the monsters or *for* the monsters.

Twitching tentacled horrors slithered along the ground, and their sharp barbs sliced and carved through the soldiers' armor. Man after man fell, but no man broke and ran, instead standing their ground and blasting away. The soldiers were dying, but they were taking their enemy with them.

The wizards and witches attempted to put up defensive shields, but the summoned horrors managed to smash through those after a few attempts. It wouldn't be long until the monsters turned on the Council.

Crazak took a deep breath and nodded to Ferrao. "We'll keep the shield up. See if you can open a portal now."

Ferrao grinned, raised his hand, and snapped. A swirling portal appeared.

Yilin rushed through it. He Who Hunts glided through next, then Crazak limped toward the portal, and Ferrao brought up the rear.

Crazak summoned a scrying window after the portal closed to watch the soldiers in their last few valiant moments, the final few succumbing to the barbs and teeth of their enemy. Only a small number of creatures remained.

If there'd been a few more soldiers, they would have won. Impressive, Army. Very impressive. It's unfortunate that you don't serve the Council.

Without magical stabilization the summoned monsters

wouldn't last more than a couple of hours before melting, but they could at least serve as a final distraction for the Council's enemies.

The elf shook his head and looked around. A third of the Council had already perished, and now the rest of them sat huddled together and wounded in a hotel room.

Crazak snorted. "Worthy foes are always the most annoying."

General Francis scrubbed a hand over his face as the gathered team read through the latest briefing documents. "Fuck."

The Deputy National Security Advisor sighed. "The President doesn't want any briefings on this matter until it's resolved."

General Black, Chief of Staff of the Air Force, shook his head. "It's not a complete failure. Our intelligence suggests we've killed at least a third of the Council, and a decent number of their support forces. Not a victory, but not a rout either."

Senator Johnston snorted. "Tell that to the families of all those men and women who died. What a damned clusterfuck! I'm going to go get something to eat. Not much point in us deciding a new course of action until we have a clue where the Council is now."

General Francis nodded. "We'll reconvene tomorrow morning to evaluate our options. We need to make sure that we have adequate intelligence before our next operation."

Everyone stood and left, downcast looks on their face as they filed out. The general begged off talking to a staffer and headed into the hallway. A few minutes later the clip-clop of high heels got his attention, and he looked back to see Senator Silvers following him.

"Can I help you?" he asked.

She sighed. "It was a good plan, General."

He snorted. "I thought you were in Johnston's camp."

Senator Silvers shrugged. "I had my concerns, but now I have different ones. I think we have all underestimated how dangerous these people are. I guess the question is what we do going forward. Johnston just seems interested in throwing more bounty hunters at it, and I'm not sure if that's wise."

The general shook his head. "From some of that drone footage we saw I think we're well past that. Imagine if those bastards had started that demon hail shit in a major city? I think we're going to need to up our game." A grim expression took over his face. "I'm going to talk about getting some backchannels going. Some of the other countries need to be brought in on this, and not just NATO allies. If we use tactical nukes in a remote area and explain why, it doesn't have to become anything more."

"*Tactical nukes*?" Senator Silvers blinked. "You think the President will sign off on those?"

The general shrugged. "Maybe. Maybe not. Maybe it's time some of us threw ourselves under the bus to defend this country. Men and women have already sacrificed their lives. If I have to sacrifice my career to stop this Council, I'm willing to do so."

"Have you mentioned this idea to anyone else?" Senator Silvers rubbed her gold ring with her thumb.

"Not yet. I want everyone to have time to stew on what happened. Sometimes you just have to offer the right plan at the right time." He shrugged. "Not even sure why I'm telling *you*. Just, you look like someone who knows that this isn't a game."

Senator Silvers gave him a nod. "I still have a few things to check on, General. Have a good night. I *will* tell you that I've been convinced of the threat. I'll voice my support tomorrow."

The general managed a smile. "Thank you, Senator."

With a polite nod, he headed down the hall. He had an appointment with his conscience and some whiskey.

General Francis sipped from his glass, shaking it and enjoying the light clink of the ice cubes. He stared out his window at the dark DC skyline. He'd sent a lot of men and women to their deaths in his career, but never without cause and without the idea that it was the best thing for the country, if not the world.

He snorted and sipped some of the whiskey, enjoying the cleansing burn as it slid down his throat. He'd had a good decade or so of service before the truth about magic and Oriceran had come out and changed everything. A lot of officers of his generation had quit, unable to handle being in the military in a time of such rapid change.

But he'd refused. If anything, it had made him want to

stay in the Army until his dying day. Magic meant new threats against the citizens he'd sworn to protect.

Too damned slow. We're still catching up. We don't even know a lot about this Council, and they're a small group. What if an entire Oriceran country *decides to come after us? What if they form some sort of alliance and invade our planet? They talk about their fancy treaties, but they still had wars that make ours look like nothing.*

A small green light in the distance caught his attention.

"What the hell is that? Drone? No, too far away."

He took another sip. The light slowly grew. Some sort of plane. Maybe even a meteor.

General Francis blinked several times as he realized that light was growing larger and coming straight at him.

The man barely had time to register the thought as a massive energy blast slammed into the side of his house and exploded. Glass, metal, and wood rained down.

7

Good times, Trey thought. *I thought we had good times as gang members, but that shit was nothing compared to this.*

He and Shorty strolled down the street, hands in their pockets. No job, no heat, no concern, just two men appreciating life.

Shorty looked at his friend and smirked.

"What's so fucking funny?" Trey asked.

The other man shrugged. "It's been a while since I've seen you in regular clothes and shit instead of suits. Fuck, *I'm* wearing a suit most of the time. Now it ain't even seem strange. Have to remind myself I ain't no business bitch."

Trey shrugged. "No crime to look good and dress good, whether you're a bounty hunter or a businessman." He grinned. "Well, maybe it is when you're as motherfucking handsome as I am." He tugged on his silk shirt. "Not that I don't still look like the handsomest motherfucker on the planet even without a suit."

Shorty laughed. "It's just weird, you know what I'm

sayin'? Last year we were hoods, and the cops were breathin' down our necks, and other gangs were fuckin' with us. Now we hangin' out with cops all the time. Other gangs don't want to be within a mile of us because they're so afraid of the Brownstone Agency's rep." He tapped his head. "You sayin' that shit don't fuck you over? It fucks with me. Not sure if it's easier or harder than bein' in the gang."

"I don't know if it's easier, with all this bounty hunting and shit, but I do feel better, and I think that's more important. All I know is that my Nana don't look at me no more with that 'You're such a disappointment, Trey' look she used to. She's proud of me now, and that's all I need to know."

A thoughtful look passed over Shorty's face. "Can I be honest with you, man?"

"Shit. You always can. Don't be pissed at me because I was right about us not doing as well at the last barbeque contest. We just need more practice, and then we'll always be taking first. I know I can be a bitch sometimes, but I was just trying to keep y'all from getting ahead of yourselves."

Most of the boys had been devasted when the judges showed up and told them they hadn't placed. Only James and Trey hadn't been surprised.

Shorty snorted. "Nah, this ain't about no barbeque shit. I guarantee we kick ass next time, though." He frowned and rubbed his neck. "It's… Fuck, man, I never thought I'd even make it this far."

"What do you mean?"

Shorty shrugged. "I joined a gang because I wanted to have a bunch of brothers to have my back, but now it's all that shit that Staff Sergeant's been fillin' our heads with. Confusin' me. Philosophy, history, and all that. It just makes me think about how I figured I could live a hard life, and it didn't matter because I was gonna be dead. Why plan for a future you ain't gonna have?"

Trey arched a brow. "And now?"

"Fuck. Now I'm all thinkin' about the money and shit I need to save for when I get married. And about how expensive college and shit is for any kids I have. We make good money workin' for the big man, but I can't do bounty hunting forever. I figure it's like pro ball, you know? We work it for a few years and save our money. But it's fuckin' weird I'm even thinkin' that way."

"Thinking about the future ain't so bad."

Shorty shook his head. "Nah, it ain't, but it's still weird, and I can't *stop* thinkin' about that kind of shit lately."

Five thugs sauntered out of a nearby alleyway and formed a line to stop the two men's advance.

Trey grinned. This would be a nice distraction for his friend.

Sometimes you just think too much, Shorty.

"Can we help you?" Trey asked, looking them up and down. No matching tattoos and they ran the range of races, including a white guy, black guy, Asian guy, Hispanic guy, and some dude Trey was pretty sure was Indian, but they all wore matching two-tone red and white bandanas around their left biceps. America the Beautiful, bringing together people in both honest and dishonest families.

Blood Tornadoes, huh? Man, these guys are fucking nothing *if they're just mugging people on the street. That's bitch-ass shit.*

The tallest of the thugs stepped forward with a grin.

"Yeah. We're collecting for a charity. We call it the Poor Brothers of Los Angeles." He shrugged. "Every donation helps." He licked his lips. "And you got some damned fancy clothes and watches. We think you could make a nice donation."

Shorty snorted. "Bitch, please. Turn your asses around before we teach y'all a fuckin' lesson."

The tall thug laughed. "You fucking kidding me? You think you can win five against two, bitch?"

Okay, got to play this the right way.

Trey nodded. "You're right. It's not a fair fight."

Shorty frowned at Trey. "What the fuck are you going on about, Trey?"

The thug chuckled. "That's right, so give us your shit. Fuck, I'll be generous. We'll just take those fine-ass watches of yours. That's real nice of us, I think."

Officers Davidson and McMillian made their way down the street on foot patrol. They were about fifty yards away from the confrontation when McMillian frowned.

He shook his head. "Damned Blood Tornadoes. I thought they would have learned their lesson after a bunch of their guys got popped last week for mugging people in broad daylight."

The cop stepped forward but stopped when Davidson put his hand on his arm. "No. Don't worry. Go ahead and call it in, because we'll need to cart them off afterward, but after that just sit back and watch this shit. It's going to be priceless."

McMillian looked at his partner like he'd lost his mind. "What the hell? We need to protect those two from the Blood Tornadoes. I'm not going to sit here and let two men be mugged right in front of me."

Davidson shook his head. "Trust me. I know those two, and the only people who are going to get hurt in the next few minutes are those dumbass gang members. They should know who they are screwing with before they start something."

Trey rubbed the back of his neck. When he had doubts about the appropriate course of action, there were a lot of people he could draw on, from Marcus Aurelius to Sun Tzu, but he had a far simpler way to decide: WWTBMD? What would the big man do?

Trey shook his head. "So, if we give you our watches you won't beat our asses?"

The thug pulled out a switchblade and popped the blade. "No, motherfucker. If you give us your watches, we won't slice your fucking faces up. Understand now?"

"I just wanted to make sure I had the right idea." Trey sighed. "There's two of us, but only five of you. That ain't fair to you, but you've pissed me off enough I don't mind beating your ass. I just wanted to make sure we didn't kick your asses when you were just asking for directions or some shit." He cleared his throat. "Last chance to turn around, assholes. I ain't paying for no broken bones."

The big man would have put you through a window by now. I'm fucking restrained in comparison.

Shorty's face broke into a feral grin.

The thugs spread out, the rest of them pulling knives.

The tall thug shook his head. "You're fucking dead, bitch. You shouldn't have had such a smart mouth."

He charged Trey and stabbed at him. The bounty hunter grabbed his arm with ease and twisted his wrist. Trey threw an elbow right into his face, and it landed with a loud thud and audible crunch.

Trey laughed. "Shorty's niece Jessica could stab a fucker harder than that. You even trying?"

The tall thug fell backward, already unconscious, his nose askew and his knife clattering on the pavement.

"What the fuck?" one of the other thugs shouted.

Shorty took advantage of the distraction to smash a powerful hook into his closest enemy. The thug's head snapped back, and he stumbled into another man. The bounty hunter rushed forward and slammed a boot into the man's stomach. The thug fell to the ground, clutching himself and groaning.

Trey delivered several savage jabs to another man, and he slumped to the ground.

"You bitches should be calling yourself the Glass Jaw Gang." Trey bounced on the balls of his feet. "And now it's down to two on two. Odds keeping getting worse. Sucks to be you."

Both of the remaining gang members flourished their knives and tried to look menacing, but their faces screamed fear.

Shorty chuckled. "You call that shit a knife? I've had bounties come at me with butter knives that were scarier."

One of the men lunged toward Shorty, who met the

man's face with his fist. The loud crunch made even Trey wince, but that didn't stop him from rushing forward to grab the final opponent's wrist and bending it back until he dropped the knife. A few stomach punches and the introduction of his knee to the man's face finished the fight.

Trey spat. "I won't defile Sun Tzu by quoting him to you bitches. Stupid dumbass motherfuckers."

Shorty shook his head. "Fuckin' trash. They should know better."

Both men tensed as two uniformed officers rushed across the street. Trey relaxed when he got a better look at one of them.

"Yo, what's up, Davidson?" he called.

The cop walked up to Trey, and they fist-bumped.

"You two okay?" the cop asked. "Didn't look like you were having much trouble, but figured I'd ask. Talk about a beatdown." He clucked his tongue and shook his head.

Shorty pointed at the unconscious gang members. "Should be askin' them. Shit, man, we ain't do nothin' but defend ourselves. We didn't even pull any weapons on these knife-carryin' motherfuckers."

Davidson shook his head and raised a hand. "Got it all on body cam, and I'm sure we can find some drone footage. Don't worry, we're taking them in. You're totally in the clear for self-defense, and we'll do all the paperwork. Don't even need a statement."

"Thanks, man."

The cop nodded to his partner. "This is my new partner McMillian. McMillian, this is Trey and Shorty, bounty hunters with the Brownstone Agency."

McMillian's eyes widened, and he barked a laugh. "Those idiots picked a fight with the Brownstone Agency?"

Davidson grinned. "I told you it'd be epic." Sirens sounded in the distance, and he nodded to Trey. "You two better get going unless you want to get caught up in paperwork shit."

The two bounty hunters waved and jogged away. They'd gotten about twenty yards when Trey frowned down at his shirt.

"*Fuck.*"

Shorty glanced his way. "What's wrong?"

"I got their motherfucking blood all over my shirt. Now I'm gonna have to get it dry-cleaned."

8

Senator Johnston shook his head as he looked around at the gathered officials. "Suffice it to say, there's a lot of cover-up going on right now. The media has more than a few questions about why the Chairman of the Joint Chiefs of Staff is dead. We poked the bear, and it decided to tear someone's head off. Maybe not surprising, but this also highlights how dangerous this Council is."

Senator Silvers sighed and shook her head. "Maybe they are too dangerous. If these Council people can just kill whoever they want with impunity, they might take us out one by one."

The Deputy National Security Advisor frowned. "There's something to be said for backing off until we have better information." He held up a hand. "I'm not saying we let them run free, just that we should consider the total risks as we formulate strategies."

Senator Johnston snorted. "The hell with that. Where I come from, if some bastard pokes you in the eye, you don't go crying to Mommy. All that teaches him is that he can get away with poking you in the eye. No, this shit means the Council is desperate, and we've now fully confirmed that they've suffered casualties and can be injured without the use of strategic-scale weapons." He slammed his fist on the table. "I'm tired of pussy-footing around so a bunch of people can look good. If you've got a nest of snakes to worry about, you send a mongoose after it. Now, here's what we're going to do. We're—"

A light breeze blew through the room, and a swirling gate appeared a few yards from the table.

The Deputy National Security Advisor shot out of his seat, along with several other officials. "Oh, my God. *It's the Council!*"

People backed away, their eyes wide with terror.

Senator Johnston stood and shook his head. "Stop embarrassing yourselves." He turned to face the portal. A Light Elf stepped out with a smile on his face.

The senator extended his hand. "Thanks for agreeing to come, Correk." He glanced over his shoulder. "If you've been reading any of the reports, you should understand that Correk has been critical to our efforts against the Council. He's far from a threat. He's the ultimate asset."

The elf shook the senator's hand. "It's my pleasure. Whatever I can do to help resolve this situation."

The panicking officials all sat.

General Black frowned from his seat. He was one of the few who hadn't stood when the portal appeared. "My understanding is that Correk's area of concern is global, not country-specific."

The elf nodded. "That is accurate, General."

"Then how do we know you're doing everything you can to help the United States?"

Correk shrugged. "You don't, but my reputation doesn't suggest I like to play pointless games. This Council is a threat, and I'm doing everything I can to help you deal with it."

The general grunted but kept his mouth shut.

The Deputy National Security Advisor cleared his throat. "Setting aside the issues of security clearances and having this man just come into our meeting without announcing him beforehand, why is he here?" He glared at Senator Johnston.

Correk smiled. "I just wanted to give you a little more insight, based on what we've seen of the Council so far. I know that some of you might be frightened by what happened to General Francis." He stepped around Senator Johnston and tapped the table twice. "But that only proves they're worried about your operations. Keep in mind that despite your awful losses, you've killed several of them and many of their trained followers." He walked behind the officials, several turning in their seats to follow him. "It's not like they can just go to the local unemployment office and grab dark wizards. I'm not trying to dismiss your losses, only remind you that this is a fight that can be won. They strike from the shadows because they have no choice."

The Deputy National Security Advisor frowned. "Are you aware of what happened during our last operation?"

"The Council ripped a dimensional hole and flooded your men with some sort of awful monsters from another dimension? Yes, I'm aware of that. I've already passed some information on to the Paranormal Defense Agency that was helpful to them stopping direct Council portals, and I'll be sending them additional information that might help cut down on similar incidents, at least in the near future. Magic isn't as precise as technology, so there are always ways around things."

General Black looked his way. "I'm wondering how secretive we should be going forward after what happened. We still don't know a lot about the Council, but if they decide to attack a major population center the casualties could run in the thousands."

Correk continued walking around the table and shook his head. "The information I've shared with your government suggests they have an interest in collecting artifacts, but not so much in mass destruction. I know you keep thinking of them as a terrorist group, but I don't believe that's accurate." He stopped behind the general's chair for a few seconds before moving on. "They've had plenty of opportunities for acts of terror. Whatever their motivation, I don't think that simply killing people is part of it, and causing a panic won't help them in their plans. My information suggests that many of the final artifacts they ended up with, although they are dangerous weapons, can be used to manipulate populations directly or indirectly. I suspect their goals are subtler than you might appreciate."

He stopped behind Senator Silvers' chair and tapped the table twice.

She frowned at him. "Why are you doing that?"

The elf shrugged. "Nervous habit. I don't like public speaking." He continued walking. "The other thing you might want to focus on in terms of investigation is magical signatures. Many spells and magical beings have a certain flavor that others can follow and detect. This might help you in your investigations and further tracking of the Council. For now, though, that's all I have to offer you."

Senator Johnston nodded slowly. "Thank you for that information."

Correk sighed and made his way to the door with a smile. "I'll make your group aware of anything else of note that I learn." He opened the door and stepped outside.

The Deputy National Security Advisor snorted after the elf departed. "That was hardly useful. He didn't tell us much we already didn't know. I appreciate his aid in these operations, but I don't want him randomly popping into our meetings."

General Black shook his head. "I disagree. I think he had a good point about their tactics, and I'm less annoyed with him than I am concerned about stopping the Council. Based on what he said, we still have some options that don't involve blowing up half a state. I wasn't all that thrilled about launching cruise missiles against targets on American soil to begin with, and I think General Francis had some more extreme ideas in mind."

There was a light knock on the door, and a moment later a couple of Secret Service agents entered, stun rods in hand. They looked up and down the table, and Senator Johnston nodded to them and then to Senator Silvers.

The agents marched behind Senator Silvers' chair. "You'll need to come with us, ma'am."

Murmurs rippled across the table.

"Excuse me?" she asked.

Senator Johnston chuckled. "Didn't you listen to the nice little briefing Correk provided?"

"What the hell are you talking about?"

"You know the part where he talked about being able to follow magical signatures? We know you're working with the Council, and those agents are going to arrest you for… well, a shit-ton of things, but first of all, aiding and abetting a group that is attempting to undermine the United States of America."

Senator Silvers shot out her seat and started rubbing the gold ring on her hand. A light green glow surrounded her.

The agents jammed the stun rods into her, and they discharged with a loud buzz. The woman fell to the ground, the glow fading. She hissed and started rubbing the ring again, but the agents shocked her several more times. She convulsed.

"Take her ring off," Senator Johnston suggested. "I don't know all that much about magic, but that might be what she needs to do it."

An agent flipped the twitching woman onto her stomach, yanked her ring off, and pocketed it.

Senator Johnston walked over and squatted by Senator Silvers. "You see, the difference between you and me is age. I've been in politics since I was twenty-one." He ran a hand through his graying hair. "Long before all this magic and Oriceran shit made things complicated policy-wise, but you know what having all that experience has taught me? That magic doesn't change much when it comes to smelling bad people. If you're going to last as long as I have, you have to be able to smell a snake."

The Secret Service agents hauled Senator Silvers to her feet. Drool ran from her mouth.

Senator Johnston pulled out a handkerchief to dry her mouth. "Let me clean you up just a bit. Cameras don't like spit too much."

"You'll…pay…for…this," Senator Silvers murmured.

He grinned. "Sure. Someday I might, but that won't change the fact that you'll be locked up." He leaned forward to whisper, "And, come on—you really think the Council's going to help someone who got caught so easily? If I were you, I'd sing for the government and ask to be hidden in the darkest, most remote hole possible. Unless you think your bosses are going to show you mercy?"

Senator Silvers' eyes widened.

Senator Johnston nodded. "Thought so."

James frowned as he scanned the obstacle course, Royce behind him. "Just wondering what we can do to improve training. Make it more realistic. Unless you think it's a bad idea?"

The DI chuckled. "I'm never going to tell you that guys can't be trained more, but I *will* tell you that you risk hurting guys if you make it too realistic. Combat readiness is an issue." He shrugged. "But I'll implement whatever training plan you want me to."

James grunted. "I know. Have to think about this shit more. Just want to…"

Trey barreled out of the back of the building. "Yo, big

man, we need you up front. We've got trouble. Fucking government's here, and the boys are ready to step up."

James nodded to Royce and jogged toward the open door. Trey led him to the front, where Charlyce was holding her hand up to a suited man with gray hair.

Fuck. That's Senator Johnston. Seen him on the news a few times, but what the fuck does he want with us?

"I'm afraid you can't go any farther, sir," Charlyce announced with a frown. "This is private property, and I've got no appointment listed for you."

Two men in suits and dark glasses who had obvious gun bulges in their jackets stood behind the senator.

Shorty, Manuel, and T.J. flanked Charlyce, glaring at the new arrivals. Several other bounty hunters filed in and looked around, frowns on their faces.

"You bitches better not be here to try and start shit over Alison," Shorty yelled. "She isn't just James' daughter anymore. She's one of us now. You fuck with Alison Brownstone, you're fucking with the entire Brownstone Agency."

The assembled men shouted their approval.

James grunted and stepped in front of his men, holding his arm out. "If they were going to do something that stupid, I doubt they'd walk in the front door." He said the words, but that didn't stop his growl. "But, tell me why the fuck you *are* here, Senator?"

9

James glared at the senator. The bounty hunter believed what he'd told his men, but that didn't mean he might not be wrong. The presence of the two armed men didn't speak to the new arrival's peaceful intentions.

On the other hand, anyone who knows anything about me knows they're not gonna be able to take me down with only two fucking men even if they're wizards, and I don't see any wands or artifacts.

Senator Johnston offered him a smile. "You and your men don't have to worry. I'm not here to cause you any trouble, son. If anything, it's the opposite. I've come to ask for your help."

James grunted. "Huh? What's with the muscle then?" He nodded to the men in sunglasses.

If this asshole wanted my help, he could have picked up a phone instead of barging into my place like he owns it. Fucking politicians.

The senator shrugged. "You're a man who hears things,

so I'm sure you've heard that we've been trying to capture the people behind the recent museum trouble here in your neck of the woods. Well, they've pushed back a little, so these two are just here for my protection." He adjusted his tie. "With that out of the way, I'd like to talk to you about that matter—the people behind the museum heist. No offense to your fine employees, but I'd like it to be in private."

The anger left the faces of the agency men surrounding them, replaced by confusion and irritation. James understood their problem. Once a man got pumped up and ready to fight, it was hard to let that anger go.

Maybe that's why it seems to charge up Whispy Doom. Maybe I'm from a planet of perpetually pissed-off men. PMS world, except for dudes. Probably just don't have enough barbeque there.

James nodded slowly. "Follow me, but your men stay here."

Senator Johnston laughed. "Fine by me. If anyone was stupid enough to attack me while I'm having a meeting with you, I'm pretty sure that would end very badly for them."

James grunted. The man had a point.

The bounty hunter led the senator down the hallway to his little-used office and motioned him inside. Once the senator was seated, James sat down behind his desk. There was no reason to waste time with bullshit posturing.

"So, yeah," he began. "I heard you were recruiting bounty hunter teams to go after the Council. You didn't come asking for me, so I didn't go asking to join up, even though I've tangled with them before and fucking *wasted* their people."

Senator Johnston nodded. "Fair enough, but we're asking now. For that matter, *I'm* asking now, son. To be honest, I wanted you from the start because of your aforementioned...wasting experience. I know you're not the only level six out there, but everything I've seen suggests you're the best in the country, if not the world. Plus, so far, you're the only man to tangle with this group and win outright. Our previous efforts haven't been the best. Good people have died. More than a few."

James frowned. "Before I even think about agreeing to help you, I need to know what you've been doing. I'm not stepping into mystery shit. That's not how I work."

"Fair enough." The senator shrugged. "We've been working closely with the Paranormal Defense Agency, along with all our own people and allied intelligence agencies. Damn, in many cases, not even *allied* intelligence agencies. There isn't a single damned country on Earth that wants some magical criminal cabal running around causing trouble. We even got a useful tip from the damned North Koreans about a possible Council site." He chuckled. "From what we've learned, they've been around for about twenty years. They formed just after all the magic started flowing back in a big way to Earth. They've got both Earth and Oriceran members. There's still a lot we don't know. We don't know what their overall goals are, but we know they've got their fingers in a lot of very shady pies, and now, thanks to their museum heist, they have several dangerous artifacts in addition to what they already had."

"So?" James shrugged. "Lots of assholes out there. Just

because these guys have magic doesn't make them special. Their people die easy enough if you take off their heads."

The senator furrowed his brow and shook his head. "Trust me, son. They've got something up their sleeve, and the fact that they already have so many little safehouses and bases set up isn't a good sign. They've been playing a long game, and we got lucky. FBI and PDA managed to capture a few mid-level agents. We made it look like they were killed. These guys play hard. Even their low-level punks don't like to be taken alive."

The bounty hunter grunted. "Yeah, I noticed that after the museum robbery."

Senator Johnston chuckled darkly. "Exactly. I'll be honest—we've done some shady shit ourselves to dig out the information we need. Deep, nasty mindreading magic, for one. Ripped information on some of their hideouts from their minds." He shrugged. "A lot of the law isn't settled on magical evidence and the Constitution, so we've taken advantage of the gray areas."

James narrowed his eyes. "Why are you telling me this?"

"Because you strike me as a man who doesn't respect bullshit, and I want to impress on you how hard it's been to get information about these people through the usual channels." The senator frowned. "The joint task force looking into this has already attempted a few extermination operations. The first you might have already heard of through your own channels. We sent in Army Special Forces backed by Paranormal Defense agents. We knew the leadership of the Council—six magicals, some from Earth, some from Oriceran—would be there. We surprised them, and our guys did a good job taking out these monsters the bastards summoned, but they had some sort of self-destruct magic. Entire team dead, and the entire site destroyed."

James grunted.

Senator Johnston sighed and shook his head. "At that point, I wanted to go to you, but the task force decided on a different plan. Two teams of bounty hunters and a Special Forces team. The idea was to distract the Council by hitting them at some of their backup locations and force them to a known rally point where our soldiers would ambush them. First bounty hunter team got slaughtered. Second team took heavy losses, but they took out one of the Council. Maybe you've heard of them—the Wu family."

James nodded. "Yeah. I've never run into them, but I've heard they are kickass bounty hunters."

"Only two of the daughters survived." The senator looked into the distance for a moment before frowning. "Those attacks were simultaneous. Even though the bounty hunters took heavy losses, the plan basically worked. The bulk of the Council was forced to their primary rally point in Montana. We distracted them with a missile barrage and then snuck in a shitload of Special Forces. Good news is that we took down a lot of their people and finished off another of the Council members, but they did some sort of crazy summoning magic. I don't know how to describe it. It was like they made demons rain from the sky. Our men were overwhelmed."

James grunted. "Yeah. I've had to deal with that kind of shit. Fucking annoying."

The senator stared at him for a moment. "You're one of the few people on the planet who could dismiss dealing with summoned monsters as just being 'fucking annoying.'"

The bounty hunter shrugged. "It sounds like you got a lot of people killed."

"Not going to deny that. Every move against these people shows how dangerous they are, and yes, a lot of good men and women are dead, but we've wounded the Council and cut down on their resources. They've lost a pile of their own people, and there're only four out of the six left." Senator Johnston pointed at James. "And this is where you come in. You're a man who gets things done. We need the biggest damned boots in the country to squash these roaches, and that's you, son. This is a level-six bounty, with the normal money accompanying it. The federal government is more than willing to pay a huge bonus, too. That'd be enough cash to swim in if you wanted. Good deal, and it doesn't hurt to earn a few favors in high places."

James snorted. "I didn't need fucking high favors when the government tried to block my daughter's adoption."

The senator held up a hand. "The government's a big entity, son. If you care about your daughter, you should help us take down these Council bastards. For all you know, they might decide to go after her next. You already stopped them once. They might harbor a grudge."

James' jaw clenched, and his hands curled into fists. "Going after my daughter would be a big mistake."

"From what I understand, their men already got on your bad side by kidnapping your girlfriend. Isn't that enough reason to go after them? If the huge amount of money doesn't sway you, I mean."

"I killed the men who kidnapped my girlfriend." James shrugged. "And who gives a shit about the money? Can't spend money if I'm dead."

"Well, now, this I didn't expect." The senator shook his head. "The Granite Ghost, the Scourge of Harriken, the great James Brownstone is afraid of someone?"

The bounty hunter locked eyes with the senator. "I'm not a fucking moron who'll toss myself into the furnace just because some politician questions how big my dick is. What you've told me is that you guys keep fucking up, and now you're desperate."

The other man shrugged. "Yes, we are, but I wanted you from the beginning. I know that if we'd had you, a lot of good men and women would still be alive."

James frowned and leaned back. He didn't give a shit about cleaning up after the government, but the Council bastards had planned an attack on LA that had ended with good cops getting killed, and they'd been prepared to kill Shay, Lieutenant Hall, and the security guards just for being in the wrong place at the wrong time.

The government's attacks had bloodied their noses, and it was as good a time as any to kick them while they were down. The senator did have a point. The Council might decide to come after James in the future because of what he'd done. He might as well take the fight to them first.

"Fine," he rumbled. "But if you want this done, I want complete support when I ask for it. Otherwise, stay the fuck out of my way. I'm not taking orders from anyone, and I don't want anyone crying if a building or two blows up by the time this is over. I'm not filing reports or asking permission for shit, either."

Senator Johnston nodded. "You just be you, son. That's what I want, and that's why I'm here. I'll make sure you get access to the relevant intelligence we've gathered."

James shrugged. "Fine, but I've got my own people who know how to find things out. I'm more interested in political help in case I *do* blow up a building. Shit like that. I also might need quick transport or portals or some shit to get to these bastards. I doubt they're going to be hanging out in LA after the ass-kicking I gave them last time."

"I'll get what you need, son. I'm no wizard, but from what I've been told, magical portals might not work again. They'll be ready for that, but if you need insertion, we'll get you there fast and in style." The senator pulled a business card out of his wallet and set it on James' desk. "If you need something, text me, and I'll get it taken care of." He pulled out a black tube with a small display and set it on the desk. "This is an authenticator. I'll be sending you information on how to access the relevant briefing files. You'll need this to access it."

James picked up the card and stared at it. "Fine. I'll take this on for now, but if I so much as smell a hint of the idea that you're fucking me over, I'll drop this monkey on your back again."

The senator shook his head. "Won't be a problem. I'm a sonofabitch, but I'm a fair one." He stood and offered James his hand. "Pleasure to work with you, son."

The bounty hunter shook the man's hand. Senator Johnston opened the door to the office and stepped out, closing the door behind him.

James took a deep breath.

Shit. Time for all hands on deck. Better have Charlyce call the Vegas team back.

He pulled out his phone and dialed Shay.

"What's up?" she answered.

"You and Peyton busy?"

"Nope. Why?"

James grunted. "Just got done talking with a senator. Negotiating, just like you told the Professor. I'm going to call Heather after talking to you. It's time to go after the Council."

"Good. I was bored anyway. I'll get Peyton going, but I think I'm going to have Lily sit this one out. She isn't ready yet for these kinds of bastards."

"Fine by me. This isn't going to be a tomb raid. This is fucking war."

Tyler sighed as he watched a blonde in a tight red dress saunter into the Black Sun. She just wasn't doing anything for him. He now preferred his women tougher, darker-haired, and in uniform.

Kathy smirked as she finished polishing a glass. "I've seen that look."

"What look?"

"Nothing." She winked. "Just the look of a man with someone in particular on his mind."

Tyler frowned and opened his mouth to offer a retort when his phone buzzed. He pulled it out and narrowed his eyes. It was a text from Brownstone.

I need the best to poke around in the dark web. Got a huge pile of cash for this one. Possible death if we fuck up though. You in? JB.

The information broker tilted his head as he stared down at the text. "What's his angle?"

Kathy stopped smirking. "Whose angle?"

"Brownstone wants my help, but he isn't exactly making it sound safe."

The brunette shrugged. "Is there money involved? Aren't you the one who's always bitching about needing to find new ways to make money off him?"

"A huge pile of cash, he says."

"Well, there you go." Kathy crossed her arms and leaned against the bar. "Then what's the problem? You like money."

Tyler frowned. "He also mentioned possible death. I kind of like living more than I like money."

She snorted. "So what? We've all got to go sometime. Don't worry, if you die, I'll make sure your bar prospers. We'll have an annual Tyler Day where we raise a glass in your honor."

Tyler rolled his eyes. "I'm sure you would."

Why should I bother? he texted back. **That shit was dangerous enough last time.**

Same guys, and it's time to finish this shit. We just got the lackeys before. Time to fuck up the people calling the shots. Don't be a pussy. Strap on a cup and saddle up.

Tyler sighed and pursed his lips. "When did I grow a fucking backbone? This shit is bad for business."

Kathy grinned. "Says the man who admits to himself he used to have a shit bar before he hooked up with Brownstone."

He glared at her. "I didn't 'hook up' with Brownstone. I just made some smart bets."

"Whatever helps you sleep at night."

Tyler snorted. "I'm probably going to be busy the next few days, if not weeks, which means you're going to be twice as busy covering for me."

Kathy shrugged. "Works for me. Means more tips. Men always tip me more than they tip you."

"That's just because you're hot."

She smirked. "Guilty as charged."

Tyler snorted and texted Brownstone again.

That pile of money better be so big I can swim in it.

Brownstone texted back immediately.

Don't worry. You'll get what you have coming. Your place, closing time.

Maria yawned. She'd read the *Homeland Security Daily Enhanced Threat Bulletin* several times. She wasn't even sure why. It wasn't a dynamic report. It wasn't as if some new local threat would spontaneously appear.

Need something to do. I'm too bored to even yell at Weber.

Her phone buzzed with a text. She looked down and furrowed her brow.

"Why is Shay texting me?"

You ready for *Night at the Museum*, part deux? Might have to go a little unofficial on this. Having a little meeting tonight to discuss it.

Where?

Black Sun, closing.

I'm at least willing to listen.

See you then, Shay texted back.

The lieutenant frowned and glanced at her watch. Her shift was over soon.

If I'm going to do this shit, I better be ready. Time to pay Dannec a little visit.

Smite-Williams was exploring the fine flavor profile of an Irish Stout when his phone buzzed with a text from James.

Okay, I'm in on the bounty. Can you offer some support?

The Professor chuckled to himself.

Much like you, lad, I don't work for free.

Last time I checked, you still owed me a few favors. And who knows what we'll find? If you want a voice at this party, you need to have fucking skin in the game.

Smite-Williams sighed. "When did this boy get so smart? I need to stop training him so well."

All right, lad. I'm in for support, and I'll put down some cash, too, but I'll need a few things in exchange.

A few seconds passed before Brownstone texted back, **We'll talk.**

James knocked on the door and waited. It didn't take that long until Zoe opened it.

The potions witch blinked several times. "Why, James, I haven't heard of you being involved in any savagery lately. What brings you to my door?" She looked him up and down, a smirk building on her face. "Is your woman working you too hard? Do you need a little pick-me-up?"

He snorted. "Nah, but that'd be funny if you could really make that happen. It'd be a good practical joke."

Zoe tilted her head, her gaze still roaming over his body and muscles. "Again I have to ask, why are you here?"

"Simple shit. I need to know how to get my hands on five hundred healing potions."

The potions witch stared at him, her mouth agape. Several seconds passed before she could muster a response. "You want *five hundred potions*? Are you planning to invade Oriceran and defeat all the Light Elves single-handedly? Who are you going to wipe out?"

James shook his head. "A certain group has gotten my attention. They're a little tougher than my normal bounties, but most of the potions aren't for me. They're for my guys, regular humans. Probably just five for me. Ten tops."

Zoe ran a hand through her hair and took a deep breath. "When would you need all these potions? You *are* aware of how expensive they'll be?"

"In about two weeks." He shrugged. "Bonus if you can get them faster, but at least get it going. The money isn't a problem. I've got plenty."

"Okay, then. You do realize I'll have to recruit aid for this job."

James nodded. "Knock yourself out. I'll pay what I need to. Just make sure I have those potions. Pretty soon a lot of people are gonna get hurt, and I want to make sure my guys survive."

"I… Very well then." Zoe sighed and shrugged.

He waved to the witch and walked back toward his F-350. She stared after him, shaking her head.

10

James looked at the crew assembled around the table: Shay, Trey, Tyler, and Lieutenant Hall. He wasn't sure about the rules concerning cops helping with bounties off-duty, but he didn't care to ask. At this point, he wanted all the help he could get.

He had just finished explaining the basic job and the fates of the previous teams. The last thing he wanted was to bullshit anyone about the danger involved.

Trey whistled. "Damn, big man, you sure know how to build up expectations. You sure even *you* haven't bitten off more than you can chew?"

James snorted. "The last time I went up against these people I didn't die. A lot of them did, and this time I'm not chasing after them worried about Shay."

Shay sighed.

Tyler shook his head. "I'll help you with collecting information, but I think this time I want to avoid following you around. I'm an information broker, not a bounty hunter."

Shay frowned. "If we're going to do this right, we need good information. We'll have to surprise them. At least from what you've said, James, these Council bastards have lost a lot of their frontline pawns, so that'll help, but this can't just be us kicking a door and hoping for the best. We need to know a hundred percent what the fuck we're walking into and be properly prepared for it."

James grunted and nodded. "Agreed. The only thing is, I don't trust this government shit, not after what happened to General Francis. According to the information the senator gave me, there was at least one person on the task force working for the Council. Who the fuck knows about spies in the Army or Paranormal Defense Agency? If there is one roach, there's always more."

Tyler nodded. "Not saying I disagree, but what's your plan then?"

The bounty hunter pointed at him. "You already mentioned it. We collect our own information. You, Heather, and Peyton. You're all used to poking the dark corners of the criminal world anyway, probably more so even than a lot of the government's spies. I'll ask the senator for help as we need it, and we've also got the Professor to check around, and he's got a lot of magical contacts."

Maria furrowed her brow. "I'll see what I can pass along. As long as it's not being held up as part of an official investigation, I should be able to at least give you some information from the national law enforcement sources." She chuckled and smiled at Shay. "This time I guess *I'm* the consultant."

The other woman grinned.

"Sounds good," James rumbled. "Yeah, to be totally clear, I don't want to do shit until we know who they are, where they are, and what we might be facing. If we can't take them out, then fuck it. We'll pass the information along to the government and they can send a dragon after their ass or something, but if we *can* take them out, we need to. That's the only way we're making money off this." He looked around at everyone. "I want this crystal-fucking-clear. These people are dangerous. If they know we're sniffing around, they might come at us. If anyone wants out, fine by me, but if you stay in, we'll take these fuckers out, and we'll make a shitload of money."

Trey cleared his throat. "I've got your back, big man. You know I do, but as much of a badass as I am, I also know that me and my boys ain't Special Forces. How are we supposed to take on magic folks?"

"You aren't. Not right away. Whatever happens, won't happen for a few weeks as we gather information. You're gonna train and help collect information in the meantime. By the time we're ready to go, you'll be better equipped to deal with magical shit. I've got a lot of healing potions coming our way, and I'll be getting you all some anti-magic deflectors. Maybe I'll talk to Zoe to see if she knows someone who can get me a bunch of them."

Trey nodded, a thoughtful look on his face.

Maria coughed. "I know a guy. He isn't exactly on the right side of the law. That said, he might provide bulk discounts, but he isn't cheap."

James grunted. "Good enough. I've got plenty of money sitting around doing nothing. Just get me the supplies I need. If he's got anti-magic bullets or other useful shit, I'm interested in buying them, too."

She laughed. "You're about to make someone really rich and yourself much poorer."

"Don't care as long as it ends with the Council dead." James stood. "Step one, we find out everything we can. Step two, we arm up. Step three, we kick their asses. Are you all still in?"

Everyone nodded.

Heather's gaze flicked to the video chat window in the corner of her second screen. Peyton stared at her with a confused look on his face.

He shrugged. "Why are you so set on video chat? What was wrong with the pure audio?"

She smiled. "Sometimes it's just nice to see what's on another person's face when you're working with them."

Peyton sighed. "Look, not trying to be a dick, but what if your kid comes through? I don't want him knowing my face. Technically, I'm supposed to be dead."

Heather laughed. "And you think Noah's going to go to his daycare and tell all his mobster friends or something?"

"Just saying."

"Don't worry. He's asleep, and he doesn't come into my room without knocking when I'm working anyway." Heather rolled her eyes.

Peyton scoffed. "I saw that."

"Hey, I'm not the one who is paranoid about a little boy selling him out." She shrugged.

"Okay, good point." Peyton looked away for a moment and then sighed. "I guess we should move forward and get to talking about how we want to handle this stuff. Unless you're hiding something very well, I'm guessing you're not a witch or magic user of any type."

Heather laughed. "Not last time I looked."

Peyton nodded. "Just double-checking. It'd be nice if we had someone like that, just to poke around some of the magical dark web stuff. I'm kind of worried these guys might not have enough of a normal presence for us to find anything useful."

"I doubt it."

"You do?" He furrowed his brow.

Heather nodded. "Yeah. At the end of the day, if they're here on Earth and buying old corporate headquarters buildings, they're going to have a presence we can follow. We just have to be smart about this. You know, examine what links the locations the government and other bounty hunters already raided, financial records, deeds—all that crap. If anything, the fact that these guys are all so obsessed with magic means they'll probably be sloppier in covering their conventional tracks."

Peyton frowned. "I don't know about that. The government has already looked pretty hard and hasn't found much."

"And you've never found something that the government thought was hidden pretty well?" She arched an eyebrow. "And you're the guy who told Brownstone you're better than me? Sad."

He scoffed. "Okay, okay, good point. Don't get ahead of yourself. We'll just divide and conquer for now. How about you hit the financials and property records related to the previous raid sites, and I'll see if I can trace any people associated with them?"

"Sounds good." Heather nodded, then let her lips curl into a slight smirk. "Don't feel bad if I find these Council jerks before you do."

Peyton smirked back. "Oh, it's on."

Tyler stared into the Manhattan he'd prepared as he leaned back in his desk chair. He brought the drink up to his lips and then set it down.

No, I need to keep a clear head if I'm going to do anything useful tonight. But what the hell am I going to do?

He snorted. He wasn't even sure why he was getting involved in this twisted mess. Brownstone had described a dangerous magical criminal organization that had slaughtered highly-trained bounty hunters and soldiers in addition to assassinating a highly-decorated military officer. The Council defined dangerous, and he'd agreed to go poke his nose into their business. He hadn't even gotten fifty percent upfront.

What the fuck was I thinking?

Tyler lifted the glass and swirled the drink, his thoughts returning to something else Brownstone had mentioned—the huge payout.

The bounty hunter was footing the bill for supplies, which meant all Tyler needed to do was provide him information. A few bribes here and there might be necessary, but his share of the bounty would make all the money he'd previously made off Brownstone seem like a rounding error.

That's all this is, nothing more than me taking advantage of Brownstone again to earn myself a shit-ton of cash. He isn't using me. I'm using him.

Tyler smirked. Not only would he earn all that money, but he also wouldn't even have to put himself in danger. The only true risk was if the Council decided to come after him, but very soon, James Brownstone was going after them. The information broker had learned long ago that only fucking brain-dead morons bet against Brownstone.

It's not dangerous, and I'm not burning any bridges. These Council assholes won't even be alive in a few weeks. No problem with earning a little money off them dying as well as earning a few points with Brownstone.

Tyler's smile disappeared. He kept trying to tell himself that helping the bounty hunter was all about the money, but something floated up from the recesses of his mind. A more burning and primal motivation: revenge.

He shook his head. The bastards had kidnapped Maria and been ready to kill her. He snorted.

I guess I'm more like Brownstone than I want to admit. Fuckers messed with my woman, so now I want to kill every last one of them. Fuck 'em.

Tyler stood and left the glass on his desk. It was time to go hit up an old friend.

11

Leaning against the cold brick wall, Tyler took a deep breath and slapped his cheeks. "Fuck, I can do this shit. He owes me a favor. He said so before. He isn't going to fuck with my mind."

The information broker stepped around the corner into the darkened alleyway.

This is a terrible fucking idea. Brownstone, you're going to get me killed or worse.

Tyler made his way toward unmarked double doors in the side of the old warehouse. A huge Kilomea in a purple suit and gold chains stood by the door. Tyler would have laughed at the huge ogre pimp's look if the Oriceran wouldn't have kicked him through a wall.

The Kilomea took a few steps toward Tyler and looked down at him, his lips curling into a sneer. "Who the fuck are you?" he bellowed. "And why shouldn't I kill you?"

Tyler's heart thundered, but he controlled his expression. He adjusted his tie before shrugging. "I'm here to see the Eyes."

"And why should I give a fuck what you want, human?"

The information broker forced a sneer onto his face. Confidence was the key to locked doors both in the legal world and the underworld.

"Because he owes me a favor. Tell him Tyler's here and wants to chat. You'll see."

The Kilomea snorted. "If he says you're full of shit I'm gonna twist you up like a pretzel." He stomped off and ducked to step inside.

Tyler let out a sigh of relief as the bouncer closed the doors behind him.

Shit. I still have time to run. Maybe I should. Maybe the Eyes was just fucking with me when he said he owed me a favor. I did give him good information, but...

The doors flew open, and the Kilomea glared from inside the smoke-filled building. "Get the fuck inside."

Tyler gave the bouncer a polite nod and entered. The Kilomea stepped outside and slammed the doors behind him.

Thick aromatic smoke choked the air and Tyler coughed a few times as he walked through the darkened hallway. As he moved, he spotted people, both humans and Oricerans, their faces locked in ecstasy as they sprawled on a couch or chair, drooling, their pupils dilated.

Tiny bands of light played across their bodies. The Eyes got something out of what he did to people, and they did, too, but Tyler was sure there was a lasting price. He was also pretty sure that more than a few of the people had stopped breathing.

I think I'll stick to booze.

Two more people in purple suits, an elf and a human,

stood in front of another set of double doors. The elf raised his hand, and a glyph appeared on his palm. He moved his hand over Tyler's chest and narrowed his eyes.

The elf held out his hand. "Give it to me."

Tyler snorted and slowly pulled out his gun, not that he thought it'd work against the Eyes. He handed the weapon to the elf.

The human guard turned and opened the door. "The Eyes will see you now."

Tyler took another deep breath and stepped inside. The smoke was even more fragrant and thick. He coughed a few more times. A single dim bulb on a chain offered the only illumination in the otherwise cramped and featureless room.

"Tyler," a voice hissed from the corner. "So nice to see you again."

He spun toward it, trying to will his heart not to explode. Two glowing solid-yellow eyes stared at him from the deep shadows in the corner.

The Eyes had a real name in his own language, but no one in the LA underworld could begin to pronounce it. The being, for its part, seemed to enjoy the fear caused by the title.

Tyler chuckled at the stray thought. He winced right after.

What have I done?

"What's so funny?" the Eyes whispered. Even though the voice was quiet and the creature remained in the corner, it sounded like he was whispering right into Tyler's ear.

"I-I just realized something. All these years I've talked

to you, I keep thinking of you as a 'he' but I have no fucking clue if that's true. I don't even know if whatever species you are has sexes."

The Eyes let out a quiet chuckle. "Think of me as whatever is most convenient. It doesn't matter." The yellow eyes vanished and reappeared in another corner. "Interesting…"

"Huh?"

"You've changed." The Eyes chuckled. "It's about time you grew a pair of balls and a backbone."

Tyler frowned. "What the fuck are you talking about? You're always confusing as fuck, but this time I don't have a clue."

The creature again winked to a different corner. "You've come because you seek information. You'll try and tell yourself it's for money, but you know it's not. I don't blame you, though. It's okay to lie to others, but just make sure you're not lying to yourself."

"I'm only about money. Just because you get off on sucking people's brains doesn't mean the rest of us mere mortals don't care about cash."

"Lies." The bulb flickered several times. "The perils of the flesh. A woman. Anger. Resentment toward those who would harm your woman."

Tyler gritted his teeth. He'd dealt with the Eyes for years, but never could be sure if the creature had magical insight or was just very good at collecting information.

The bartender sighed. "If you already know all this, then you know why I'm here."

The Eyes disappeared. Tyler frowned after several seconds and looked back and forth. He turned around to find the solid-yellow eyes staring right into his mere inches away.

He yelped and stumbled back. "*Fuck.*"

The creature laughed, a wheezing and unsettling sound. "Humor me, Tyler. I enjoy the taste so much."

"The taste of what?"

"Tell me about the woman first," the Eyes insisted. "That's my price."

Tyler sighed. "Okay. Shit. I admit it. I fell for someone, a cop. How is that for fucking irony? I wasn't even looking, but, yeah. I'm here to ask about the Council. They fucked with her, so they pissed me off, and so I'm doing some shit I probably shouldn't. At the rate I'm going, I'll probably be a cop by next year. That enough?"

"Yes," the Eyes hissed. "More than enough. Interesting and wrong."

"Huh? What do you mean wrong?"

The creature vanished again. Tyler waited several seconds before turning around. This time the Eyes was back in the corner.

"You move in her direction, but she also moves in yours."

Tyler shrugged. "Not going to say she doesn't push the line every now and again."

"You will find equilibrium." The creature wheezed more laughter.

Tyler frowned. "What do you mean?"

"That is the way of the universe. Equilibrium. The woman motivates you, but you're here for another reason —because some have forgotten the equilibrium that defines existence. The forces of darkness are making a large play. Their counter has already gathered and will deliver a terrible blow."

"Okay, I like the sound of that. You're saying we're going to win this?"

"Perhaps. The Council is wounded and unprepared for what you're bringing." The Eyes offered another wheezing laugh. "I'm no seer. I just know the present. I can tell you that your lance of stone is more powerful than you can possibly imagine."

"Lance of stone? Oh, I get it." Tyler snorted. "Yeah. I wouldn't bet against him."

"I will give you more. I know much about them, but there's a price."

"I thought you said you owed me?"

The Eyes winked to another corner. "Special information has higher value and a higher price. You will bring me someone."

Tyler furrowed his brow. "Huh? Bring you someone? What do you mean?"

"Bring me someone. They must be alive. I have need of their body. You don't need to know why."

Tyler couldn't keep the disgust from bubbling up to his face.

The Eyes zoomed forward until the creature was right in front of him. The faintest ripples in the air suggested a shuddering and twisting form barely connected to reality.

"Don't give me that look, Tyler," the creature hissed. "Many servants of the darkness will fall in coming days. Just keep one alive and bring him to me. If you do, I'll provide you with useful information on your enemies.

"Done." Tyler swallowed and turned to leave. There really were things worse than death.

James nodded to himself as he looked around the table in the briefing room at Camp Brownstone. Trey, Dannec, Lieutenant Hall, and Shay sat in front of computers poring over the government reports and trying to cross-reference them with the clues provided by Heather and Peyton. For now, their focus was on the magic used by the Council. That magic was what was letting the Council win in fights. His team needed to figure out a way to neutralize it.

We've got a good start on this shit. Just need to make sure we're prepared.

Dannec frowned and shook his head. "Anti-magic deflectors will be somewhat useful, but you're going to need more than that. These four-armed creatures they keep using—they're called Zain. They aren't demons; you can think of them as secretive but dumb magical mercenaries. Pure anti-magic won't do much, and they're able to rip through most metals with ease with their claws." He rubbed his chin and grinned. "If you have the money, I'm sure I could find some additional defensive magical artifacts to sell you. I'll gladly grant you a discount for purchasing in bulk."

Trey snorted.

James shrugged. "I've got the money. Not like I've got anything better to spend it on."

Shay pointed at a still from a drone video. A four-armed monster lay on the ground, bleeding out. "Looks like they aren't bulletproof."

Dannec nodded. "They're extremely tough, but regular weapons can kill them. They can take a lot of punishment before going down, though."

The tomb raider grinned. "Sounds like an excuse for me to crack out the high explosives and machine guns. I don't always get to play with the big toys."

Lieutenant Hall glanced her way and snorted. "I guess I shouldn't be surprised that you have that kind of stuff considering what you…used to do."

James frowned but said nothing. The cop already knew about Shay's past, which might complicate things if she decided she didn't like a former hitman wandering the country with illegal weapons. He also didn't want Shay's past leaked to his men just yet. If Trey found out, it'd be hard for him to keep his mouth shut. Then again, a bunch of former gang members probably wouldn't care.

Hall knew the fucking score. She didn't have to volunteer to join if she was gonna have a problem with Shay being Shay.

Trey looked at the two women and shook his head. "Shit, I don't even want to know about whatever cat-fight shit's about to start."

Shay's smile faded. "Is that going to be a problem, Maria? I don't know about James and his men in terms of what they're allowed to have, but I don't plan on going after the Council with just a 9mm and a few strategic f-bombs."

Trey and Dannec chuckled. James grunted, not bothering to hide the annoyance on his face.

Lieutenant Hall pointed at Dannec. "Considering how

much I've dealt with him, I can't say shit. Glass houses and all that. I can't exactly lecture anyone on always following the law anymore. One thing this year has taught me is that sometimes you just have to step over the line to protect people. Fucking brass seems more concerned about appealing to politicians than making sure AET gets shit done or saves anyone." She grinned. "Anyway, I'm here not as a cop, but as a consultant. I can compartmentalize for my clients."

The tension left James' shoulders and neck, and he turned to Dannec. "So, anti-magic deflectors, some sort of magic shields and armor. Anti-magic bullets. I want it all. Like I've been saying, this isn't a bounty. This is war, and I want to go to war with good equipment."

The elf nodded. "Of course, Mr. Brownstone. I'm more than happy to supply you with whatever you need, provided your money keeps flowing."

The bounty hunter grunted. "You don't even give a shit that I'm taking on the Council, do you? You just care that I'm dumping a shitload of cash on you."

Dannec shrugged. "They'll eventually be bad for my business, but I've been thinking about taking a long vacation soon, and draining you dry might help with that."

Trey laughed. "Damn, man, you ain't hiding shit."

"I encountered a wonderful human saying the other day. 'Don't hate the player, hate the game.'"

"I like it better that way," James rumbled. "We don't have time to fuck around with this. If everyone's honest, it makes shit simpler."

Trey adjusted his tie. "Well, if I'm honest, I want a bigger fucking gun. I ain't want to go after no wizards with my big mouth and a 9mm either. If the cops are looking the other way, it's time to get motherfucking serious firepower. A man's gun says a lot about him, you know what I'm saying?"

His boss groaned. Shay smirked.

James shrugged. "Why the fuck not? Just think of it as an early Christmas bonus."

12

Crazak shook his head as he slipped into his chair. Looking around the table, no one would be able to tell that not all that many days prior the Council had been fighting for their lives. The survivors' wounds were healed, and their current clothes immaculate. Still, the frowns and suspicion on their faces spoke of their experiences.

The elf summoned a few quick scrying windows. Their surviving safehouses and bases had not yet fallen.

"We've suffered losses, but we're not defeated. I can see now that being overly reliant on establishing ourselves in the United States was perhaps shortsighted, but that doesn't change the fact that we can't reverse twenty years of planning."

Yilin frowned. "We need more information on where the government pawns might strike next. All my contacts have been useless."

Ferrao drummed his fingers on the table. "The loss of Senator Silvers has made us even blinder. Still, she lacked access to all of the information we needed. Even *she* didn't seem to know how the government had learned the locations of our facilities."

Yilin snorted. "Useless anyway. Warning us about the first raid was helpful, but she did little to help us with the others."

"The military forces kept the operational details from much of the committee." The gnome shrugged. "She'd at least told us enough that we could reinforce our facilities, and the trap at our first facility has bloodied the government's nose. It doesn't matter anyway. They have her now."

He Who Hunts shook his head, his face, such as it was, hidden by his cowl. "I've tasted the magic at the sites. Our enemies did not trace us using magic. They knew where to strike."

"Lawrence's and Elizabeth's contacts remain to be exploited," Crazak offered, "but we still have to establish all the people they were dealing with. That will take some time."

The secrecy that protected the Council also hurt them.

Yilin's frown slowly faded. "Perhaps it's over."

"Over?"

She nodded. "Yes. They struck us repeatedly at our secret bases ferociously, but they've not followed up since then. Perhaps the slaying of General Francis was sufficient to cow them."

He Who Hunts laughed. "Foolish hope doesn't become foolish reality just because we cling to it."

Yilin's face contorted in rage. "Do you have something useful to add?"

"Blood has been spilled, but you forget that they are not as ruthless as we are." A raspy laugh followed.

Crazak nodded. "They've hit us hard, but they've taken heavy casualties. They will need time to pick up the pieces, which provides us with an opportunity to better fortify our position. We will keep looking into the government's efforts. We should abandon this place and keep on the move. That will slow them down." He looked at He Who Hunts. "And take care of Senator Silvers. We can't have them getting any information from her."

He Who Hunts let out a hollow, raspy laugh. "It will be my pleasure."

Senator Silvers paced her cell, rubbing her wrists. It'd only be a matter of time before a more severe interrogation began. It was only her status as a senator that was preventing the government from using the dirtier methods they might otherwise leverage in an investigation of the Council. They'd tried conventional interrogation, but she'd continued to insist she'd been framed by Correk.

They think they can scare me. They don't understand who I work for.

If only I had my ring. These fools don't even have this place well-secured against magic.

She scrubbed a hand over her face. If she could escape, she could at least beg the Council's forgiveness. She'd given them useful intelligence and helped them hurt the government forces. It wasn't her fault that she'd been captured. They had to understand that. She couldn't have anticipated Correk's trick.

A loud alarm sounded, and muffled shouts echoed through the hallways.

Senator Silvers rushed to the door to peer through the small window but couldn't make anything out. There were no other prisoners in this part of the facility, but obviously, something was going on.

It's my chance. I have to take advantage of it. But how?

A cold wind blew past her and goosebumps formed on her skin.

What was that?

A tremor shook her body, and her heart sped up. She slowly turned around.

Red eyes stared out at her from a hood.

Senator Silvers took a deep breath. "Master, you've come to rescue me. I promise you that I've told them nothing." She managed a smirk of pride. "And even if you left me here, I'd continue to tell them nothing. I'm a loyal servant of the Council."

"Yes," He Who Hunts whispered. "You will be left here, and you will continue to tell them nothing."

A misty red arm shot out and wrapped around her neck.

The senator didn't even have time to scream before her head melted.

Dannec smiled as he surveyed the pile of artifacts on a table in his living room. This little war on the Council would make him a very wealthy man.

Who would have thought helping the good guys would prove so profitable?

His smile faded. In searching through the information provided by the government, he'd found a few references that didn't sit well with him. He'd not wanted to disturb Brownstone's little task force until he had better information. A major part of the mystique of his job was looking like he knew more than others even when he didn't.

These Council fools are playing with dangerous magic, even for them.

Alarm spells whispered in his ear. Someone was opening a portal directly into his apartment.

Dannec grabbed a horn from his mantle and chanted a quick spell. The horn burst into a blue flame.

I'm not such easy prey, Council.

The portal opened, and Correk stepped out.

The Fixer eyed the horn with a raised eyebrow. "That's overkill, don't you think?"

Dannec set the horn back on his mantle, and the flame extinguished itself. "Better overkill than being killed, I'd say."

Correk chuckled. "I see you're as subtle as ever." He glanced around the room. "And business is good."

"It'll be even better soon, thanks to Brownstone." Dannec dropped into a nearby recliner. "Are you here to shut me down, Fixer?"

The other elf shrugged. "If you give me a reason to, but today's not the day. I'm here because you asked me here."

"I was expecting you to knock."

"You've been spending too much time around humans."

Dannec laughed. "What an odd thing to say, especially coming from you."

"Perhaps." Correk found a nice seat on the couch. "Very comfortable."

"I try."

A tense silence passed between them for a long moment until the Fixer finally cleared his throat.

"I never supported your exile, you know. You were right to not obey those orders. Innocent humans would have died. It was wrong of them to suggest secrecy was more important than life."

Dannec looked down. "They still saw me as a traitor who would put humans before Light Elves. Who knows, maybe they were right." He looked back up. "It doesn't matter. I've made a comfortable life for myself, and the way things are continuing, I imagine that soon *all* of us will be living among humans. If half of what people say is true, Oriceran doesn't have long."

"Rumors and whispers, not facts. And 'soon?' Do you mean by human or elf standards?"

"Both." Dannec grinned. "But enough of the past, Fixer. I didn't contact you to talk about my banishment. I came to terms with that long ago. I needed your help with Brownstone."

Correk furrowed his brow. "Yes, Brownstone's fight against the Council. You mentioned wanting my advice in your message?"

Dannec nodded. "The Council seems fond of Zains, but there was an offhand reference in one of the interrogation records. The humans thought it was mere babble, but it sounded familiar to me. I realized the word was old

Atlantean, which was why they thought it was gibberish. I translated it, but I still don't know what it means. Do you have any idea what a soul drinker might be?"

Correk frowned deeply. "Soul drinkers? Nasty creatures, but they're extinct. There hasn't been one spotted on Oriceran for millennia."

The other elf shrugged. "It is clear to me that the Council has at least some."

"Perhaps it's not so surprising. Brownstone killed a similar monster in Japan, but they were calling it a despair bug. The soul drinkers might have been hiding on Earth all this time." Correk frowned. "So many dangerous things are making themselves known now."

"Sounds like a job for the Fixer."

Correk nodded and stood. "If they can't be reasoned with, then yes, but for now, this is more your problem. I'll get you some tomes from the Library. They might prove useful in dealing with these creatures." He lifted his hand, and a portal appeared. "If you *could* come back to Oriceran, would you? This Council represents a threat to both Earth and Oriceran. I'm sure your involvement in its defeat could convince certain parties to rescind your exile."

Dannec shrugged. "Don't misunderstand. I'm helping Brownstone and his friends first and foremost for money. My time in exile has made me far less idealistic than I once was."

The elves stared at each other for a moment, then Correk smiled. "Your choice." He stepped through the portal.

"Yes, Correk. It *is* my choice."

Trey opened the back door of his F-350 and shoved the handcuffed bounty inside. A level one wasn't even worth his time anymore, but the big man insisted that the agency make at least some apprehensions so the scum of LA wouldn't get too brave. A quick bag-and-tag was nice anyway, like a brisk jog that got a man's muscles loose.

Got to keep the skills going.

He slammed the door shut and hurried to the driver's seat.

"You don't have to do this, pal," the disheveled bounty slurred from the back. His fetid breath should probably be classified as a chemical weapon by the UN. "I can pay you more than my bounty, you know. You can make a sweet profit. No paperwork, even."

Trey snorted and started his truck. "Bitch, please. You think you can bribe the Brownstone Agency? You must be high, in addition to being drunk."

"Whatever, pal. You're a bounty hunter. You're just a prick who arrests other people for money. Don't act so high and mighty."

Trey pulled away from the curb. "You seriously think you're gonna guilt-trip me into letting you go? Keep dreaming."

The bounty shook his head. "Nah, asshole, listen to what I'm saying. I'm gonna bribe you. So what if I took a little money that didn't belong to me? They were giving it away to a bunch of cripples anyway. Anyone would have done what I did."

Trey glared into his rearview mirror. "That was a

charity for wounded veterans, you motherfucking piece of shit. Don't tempt me to pull this truck over and beat your ass."

"Just saying. It's like Scrooge said. Those assholes should just die and deplete the surplus population."

Trey snorted. "Keep talking like that. I know one way to deplete the surplus population." His phone rang, and he snatched it from his pocket. "What?" he snapped without looking at the caller ID.

"Don't you take that tone with me, Trey Garfield," Aunt Charlyce hissed back.

"Oh, I'm sorry." He winced. "The bag-and-tag was annoying me. Didn't even know who was calling."

"I'll tell your Nana on you if you keep that up." She muttered something in her throat. "Anyway, after you're done dropping off the bounty, Mr. Brownstone wants you to stop by and pick up the first set of the healing potions. He says you don't have to worry about the money. He's taken care of that. He just wanted to make sure someone reliable did it because he's busy with all this research and whatnot."

"Yeah, yeah, fine. I'll do it."

"All right, then. Don't be so rude next time."

Trey chuckled. "I won't, Auntie Charlyce." He ended the call and looked into the rearview mirror. "I need to hurry and drop your ass off. I've got better shit to do than ride around with some stanky-ass motherfucker."

13

Trey whistled as he strolled up to Zoe's door. He knocked lightly and waited, his hands in his pockets.

I still can't get the smell of that asshole's breath out of my nose.

The witch opened the door, her white robe clinging to her wet body, her dark hair sticking to her face.

Okay, that's a nice distraction.

Trey looked her up and down. "Did I come at a bad time?"

Zoe shook her head and grinned. "Nope. Just took a little shower. Helps sometimes when I have a hangover." She motioned him inside. "I was trying something different today." She twirled around. "Don't worry, I assure you I'm sober right now."

"Yeah, okay, then." Trey shrugged. "Not really my business, ma'am."

The bounty hunter stepped into the maze of standing and hanging planters filled with a variety of plants, including several that were twitching, moving, or glowing.

A riot of smells attacked his nose, but he couldn't say anything smelled bad, especially compared to what he'd been dealing with earlier.

The witch closed the door and sashayed toward the kitchen. She stopped before entering and turned around, her gray-eyed gaze roaming over Trey's body.

Is she checking me out?

"Big man should have called ahead," Trey explained. "I'm just supposed to grab some of the potions. You got a box, or do I need to go get one?"

Zoe marched away from the kitchen and behind Trey.

He started to turn to face her.

"Don't turn," she ordered.

"Huh?"

What the fuck is going on?

"I'm looking at something," Zoe explained.

Trey frowned. "What?"

"Your nice ass." She laughed.

Trey's brow lifted. "Not that I'm complaining. It *is* a mighty fine ass, but, damn, girl, you sure you're not smashed? Big man told me how much you have to down for your magic."

She wagged a finger at him. "Not in the slightest, which is unusual for me." She chuckled and ran a hand down her side. "You know, I could make this whole thing a bit cheaper for your boss."

"Okay." Trey shrugged. "I'd have to call him. I don't make the decisions on the big expenditures."

Zoe tittered. "No, no. You don't understand. You'd be the one giving me something. It doesn't involve him at all."

Her eyebrows raised suggestively. "I follow the Dionysian Way. Do you understand what that means?"

"Yeah, I get that. It means you're into the wine for your magic."

"Yes, that's part of it, but many followers of Dionysus aren't just interested in wine. There are certain activities that are just as intoxicating." After a few seconds, Zoe licked her lips.

Trey's eyes widened in surprise.

Is this shit happening? What is it with hot witches eyeing me? Not that I'm gonna complain.

He cleared his throat. "So, you're saying we have a little fun, and you cut down on the big man's bill? I mean, you're damn hot, so I'm not exactly saying you'd have to do that anyway, but since you already mentioned it, I want to do my professional due diligence."

Zoe inhaled deeply and then slowly let it out. "Yes. Sex with a virile man offers great power."

Trey straightened his tie. "Ma'am, I guess if I have to sacrifice my virginity for the team, I'm your man."

He winced and had no idea why he'd just admitted that to the witch.

Dumbass, Trey. What the fuck are you doing?

Zoe blinked. "Your virginity?" She gasped and put a hand over her mouth. "How perfect. How utterly perfect. You don't even realize the value of what you've offered me."

Trey laughed and shrugged, some of his embarrassment fading. "Well, I've been trying to save it for someone special, and a witch is pretty damned special."

"Oh, indeed. I'm one WILF you'll enjoy sharing your

first time with." She headed toward her bedroom, hands on her hips. "Although it's an amusing joke, young man."

"You ain't that much older than me, and it ain't no joke."

"Sure." The witch looked over her shoulder. "As for my age, let's just say I aged well." She winked. "If you're telling the truth, you're about to save your employer millions of dollars."

The bounty hunter laughed. "Damn, I'm the kind of gigolo you have to save up for."

Trey followed her into the bedroom. She dropped her robe and closed the door with a grin.

Heather blinked at the grinning Peyton in the video chat window. "Cleaning service? Seriously?"

He nodded. "Yeah. They used the same company, and it doesn't have any links to Purity or any of the other underworld companies handling that kind of crap. Only a small number of companies are using it."

Heather nodded. "Okay, I've identified a few of the shell companies they've been using. If we cross-reference those shell companies with some of the cleaning company stuff, we might be able to pinpoint a few more of their bases." She tapped away at her keyboard. "Sending you the most likely hits."

Peyton picked up a piece of pizza and took a bite. He demolished it before nodding. "We're actually kicking ass and taking names. It looks like the Council's hacker game just isn't as good as their magic game." He set down his slice of pizza and clicked his mouse a few times. "Cross-referencing the data now, and...bingo. Looks like we got two strong hits." He grinned. "Perfect."

Heather frowned. "Care to share with the rest of the class?"

"Easy targets." He laughed. "One's in Vegas, and the other is a little outside Salt Lake City. It's like they're begging for Shay and Brownstone to go kick their asses."

Heather picked up her phone. "Okay, send me the information. I'll let James know."

Trey rested his head against the headboard of Zoe's bed, a stupid grin on his face.

Yeah, damn! Don't know if it was smart to have waited so I could share it with someone like her, or if I've been denying me some fine-ass fun all these years.

The witch lay on her back, covered in sweat, pale, her eyes wide. "Amazing."

Trey laughed. There wasn't an ounce of tension left in his body, and he decided to switch fully over to Smooth Trey. Not much point fronting linguistically with a powerful witch he'd just fucked.

He shrugged. "I don't like to brag, but I'm pretty damned good at everything I do. I think this is just more proof of that."

Zoe sat up, blinking a few times and swaying unsteadily. "I just thought you were joking. I never imagined it was true."

Trey furrowed his brow. "Joking? What about having punched my V card?"

"But you were a *virgin*." Zoe shook her head and brushed the hair out of her eyes. "Please don't be offended, but the men you associate with don't strike me as the type who would tolerate such things without mockery."

Trey shrugged. "Yeah, not saying they would, but they didn't know."

"How did you keep it a secret?"

He laughed. "Not like they had a way to check." He pounded his chest. "And who would believe a young, virile, handsome badass like myself hadn't dipped his wick?" He smirked at the witch. "Hell, apparently even *you* didn't believe it, and I figured you would be able to tell with your magic and shit."

"I could after we started, but not before." Zoe took a few deep breaths. "You're unusual."

"I prefer awesome, but I'll take unusual."

"You don't understand. The level of power I've received from sleeping with you is beyond what I'd expect even with a virgin, and for that matter, you did demonstrate a certain amount of natural talent that had nothing to do with magical potential."

Trey laughed. "Got to give credit to my years of internet studies for that."

Zoe fell back on the bed, her hand over her chest. "Thank Dionysus I was sober for this. I…need… I want more from you in the future. It hasn't been that fantastic for me for a long time, and even without the virginity, it'll be glorious. I'm going to need more of the Treymeister."

He smirked. "That's what they all say."

She gave him a quizzical look.

"Well, that's what they all say in my dreams, anyway."

Trey rolled out of bed. "I'd love to stay and rock your world all night, but I was just supposed to stop by and pick up those potions. I need to be getting back to Camp Brownstone to check in with the big man."

Zoe sighed and nodded. She hopped out of bed and walked over to her dresser. Trey couldn't help but stare at her naked, fine ass as she did.

She opened the dresser, pulled out a locket, and tossed it to him.

He snatched it out of the air. "What's this?"

"A charm. Defensive magic. It won't stop the most powerful spells, but I'd hate to be your first and last." Zoe gave him a somber look.

Trey looked down at the locket, which was a small gold circle inscribed with a rune. "This isn't going to make me a mind-zombie, is it?"

The witch chuckled and shook her head. "Not any more than nature and your instincts, now that you've tasted the nectar."

"It's all right. The big man trusts you, which means I trust you."

The witch shivered.

"What's wrong?" Trey asked.

"I…I've no intention of mistreating you, but I now realize that James might take it personally if I don't treat you right."

"I don't need the big man to be my chaperone." He winked.

The witch rummaged through her dresser and pulled out a small white bottle. She opened it and sprinkled the contents over her hand. She placed her hand over her heart. "I swear to Dionysus that I will only be truthful to you."

"I appreciate it, Zoe."

Her hand started glowing, and the light surrounded her whole body before fading.

Trey blinked. "What the fuck was that?"

"A true oath. My honesty is now assured."

"Damn. Well, that's good. That's the only way I'd work with you. Honesty up front saves a lot of misunderstanding."

Zoe picked up and slipped on her robe. "Let's go get you the first box of potions. I meant what I said about cutting the price. You don't have to tell James the reason if you don't want to."

Trey grinned. He didn't think he'd mention the virgin thing, but mentioning how he'd slept his way to a multi-million dollar discount wasn't such a bad thing in his mind. "Okay, then. Thanks for doing business with Team Brownstone."

The witch smiled. "Tell James I'll have the next batch in forty-eight hours."

14

A few days later, a Ford Expedition rumbled along the street, with Trey driving. He drummed his fingers on the wheel and smiled.

It's good to be alive.

"Why you grinnin' like a fool?" Shorty asked from the front passenger seat.

Trey snorted. "What the fuck you talking about? How am I grinning like a fool?"

Shorty shrugged. "The last few days you've been grinnin' like you won the lottery or somethin', but I ain't heard shit from you that tells me why that'd even be."

"What, a man can't just be happy? I've got good friends, a good job, and I'm damned handsome. Don't be such a hater, Shorty."

"I'm just sayin' it's mighty suspicious is all, you know what I'm sayin'?"

Deshawn laughed from the middle seat. "Yeah. It depends on what he's happy about."

Trey snorted.

Glad I didn't tell these motherfuckers anything about what happened with Zoe. They wouldn't understand why it was a beautiful fucking thing.

"Worry less about me and more about the bounty," he explained. "This fucker's a level three, and we're going into his fucking turf. Don't know what tricks he's got. Plus, the big man wants us to practice with the non-lethals, which is why he gave us all those healing potions to use—just in case the non-lethals don't go so well on our end."

Shorty shook his head. "We still might get motherfucking shot."

"But you won't die," Deshawn insisted.

They had a solid team assembled: Trey, Shorty, Deshawn, Isaiah, Lachlan, and Max. Several level threes had popped up in the last couple of days, and James wanted them taken down as soon as possible. Apparently, even a minor easing up by the agency had convinced some scum they were free to pop out of their holes.

Got to keep fumigating.

James had purchased some stun rifles and stun rods. Their limited effective range made them something he'd normally want the men to avoid, but he thought it'd be a useful exercise in pushing them to their limits when the enemy was using more powerful weaponry. This was all part of his effort to get them ready to help take on the Council.

We'll show these fuckers why they better not screw with the Brownstone Agency, even when we're not here to gun their punk asses down.

Trey turned onto a pothole-covered street, wincing with each shudder of the vehicle and wondering what it was doing to the suspension. The Expedition wasn't his beloved F-350, but he still didn't like the idea of damaging an official Brownstone Agency vehicle on a job. Professionals didn't get their wheels damaged. Punk-ass bitches did.

"If we corner Howard, he shouldn't be all that, but the word is he's got himself some guards. This shit ain't dead or alive, but you do what you need to protect yourself, and remember the big man wants this to be a practice with this stun shit." He glanced into his rearview mirror with a frown. "Please tell me you dumbass motherfuckers all have your healing potions?"

They all patted their pockets and nodded.

Trey nodded. "Good. Those ain't for scrapes, but they'll save your life. He paid a shit-ton for each one, so every time you use one you're wasting his money."

And wasting my bedroom skills.

Shorty snorted. "I ain't need no magic potion. Best way not to need it is to just shoot the other motherfucker first. Don't matter if it's a stun rifle or a Glock."

Trey slowed the Expedition. They were almost to the abandoned apartment complex. The bounty had turned the area into his own little criminal office space. Fortunately, that also meant that most people who were not part of his posse knew to avoid the area. Even in one of the roughest parts of town, people didn't seem very interested in getting caught up in trouble.

James had stressed increased safety despite wanting them to use non-lethals. Everyone had a potion and a bulletproof vest. Trey understood his intention. The boys had gotten used to easy beatdowns, but the Council wouldn't be drunk losers they could manhandle, even with better weapons.

Staff Sergeant Royce had stressed it too. Warrior protection was a mindset, he said. If the men got too cocky, someone might end up dead. Healing magic could do a lot, but it couldn't bring you back to life.

Don't matter. If any of us were supposed to die, it would have happened when we were running in the gang. We've got a second chance, and we're on the right side.

Trey parked the SUV on the street and looked over his shoulder into the backseat. "Lachlan, you're gonna guard our wheels. Anyone gets near 'em, stun their asses. That shit lasts a while."

The other bounty hunter frowned. "What the fuck? Just lock it. I ain't need to watch it."

Everyone snorted.

"What?"

Shorty shook his head. "I can't believe the bitch who once wanted to jack Brownstone's wheels says we should leave a fine-ass vehicle just sitting around to get stripped. Guard the damned SUV, Lachlan. I don't want to cram into some Currus or shit like that."

The younger man snorted. "Just saying, I want to beat their asses down, too." He crossed his arms and muttered under his breath, a petulant expression on his face.

Everyone else exited the SUV and marched up the street behind Trey in a loose gaggle—five fit young men in suits. A random person might have mistaken them for being on the way to the business conference if they hadn't been walking up a cracked sidewalk past several junkies shooting up and buildings with barred and boarded-up windows. That and the stun rifles slung over their backs.

A drunkard in an alley looked at them, a bottle of whiskey in hand. "Hey, I didn't do it, officer."

Trey snorted and shook his head. "We ain't no cops."

Fuck. Our neighborhood was never this bad. Was that because James lived there?

A few minutes of additional walking didn't improve the local sights, but it did bring the bounty hunters to an abandoned apartment complex. Almost all the windows had been boarded up, and a large number of tags covered the buildings. The parking lot was cracked and filled with holes, and weeds had taken over both it and the sidewalks around the single-story complex.

The unkempt nature of the buildings and parking lot didn't match all the souped-up and customized cars in the parking lot. The juxtaposition of the sad state of the complex and the expensive vehicles was striking.

Seems like our guy doesn't keep his home clean, and his boys aren't doing much to keep a low profile.

The bounty hunters went from the parking lot into the inner courtyard connecting all the apartments.

Trey narrowed his eyes as he took in the tags. The Bay Boys. Stupid name for a small gang, but they were vicious enough. He'd never tangled with them back in his gang days, if only because the bastards had been based so far from his gang's territory.

"We know Howard's here," Trey announced, "but I guess we're gonna have to smoke him out apartment by apartment. Remember, once you stun a fucker and the room's secure, use the zip-ties because that stun ain't gonna last more than a few minutes. They'll be woozy when they get up, but that ain't mean they can't shoot your asses."

Deshawn looked around the area. "What if he runs?"

Trey shook his head. "He won't run. He isn't the type. He's a wannabe cartel leader. Maybe he'd run from the big man, but not us."

A few shadows moved near the windows of several of the apartments. They were being watched.

Here we go. Here we go.

Shorty shrugged. "If he thinks he's such a badass, let's call him out. It'll make it easier. I don't want to waste a lot of time playin' hide and seek.'

Trey frowned. He didn't have to consider Sun Tzu or any of the other military commanders they'd read to think that was a bad idea. They had intelligence on their target, but no knowledge of his exact location and the strength of the local forces. Stirring them up was a bad idea.

"Yo, Howard, you small-dick piece of shit," Shorty shouted. "We got somethin' to say to you, so you better get your weak-kneed piece-of-shit ass out here right now and stop wastin' our motherfuckin' time."

Trey rounded on the other man. "What the fuck, man? That was *not* the motherfucking plan."

Shorty shrugged. "Just speedin' this shit along. Why waste time?"

The other bounty hunters laughed. Trey sighed and shook his head.

The sound of several doors opening echoed around them. Tough thugs stepped out from the apartments, their guns prominently sticking out of their pants. Their gang colors confirmed they were Bay Boys.

Within fifteen seconds, twenty armed gang members stood in the courtyard.

Trey slapped Shorty upside the head. "This is why you don't do that kind of shit." He glared at the other men. "Let's play it cool."

The Bay Boys parted, and a tall, muscular man in a white suit strode forward, their target, Howard. He flashed a smile, revealing a gold tooth.

Now that shit is just tacky, but it looks like the Boys are working for him and not just hanging out in his territory. Damn.

Howard crossed his arms. "I hear someone has something to say about my dick. It couldn't possibly be one of you little bitches, because there aren't enough of you to take out all the guys who work for me, fancy suits or not." He snickered. "Stun rifles? Please. No one's afraid of a fucker who is too afraid to kill them.

Trey adjusted his tie and stepped forward. "I'm Trey Garfield with the Brownstone Agency."

"And you think I should give a shit? You already know who I am, which is why you're here, but you've made a really stupid mistake, asshole."

The bounty hunter frowned. They were outnumbered and on open ground. Even with their vests, there was too much of a chance of a headshot. It was time to draw on his inner Sun Tzu.

On hemmed-in ground, resort to stratagems.

Trey nodded to his men. "Come on, boys, let's go. Time for a strategic withdrawal." He winked when his back was turned and mouthed, "Use the fucking cars as shields."

Several of the men frowned, but Shorty grinned. "Yeah, let's go. Howard's just too much man for us."

"That's right, assholes," Howard shouted. "It's good to understand who the real big dick is around here. Fucking pissant bitches."

The bounty hunters turned to leave, moving among a few of the cars.

Trey ducked behind some purple-painted monstrosity with huge wheels and yanked around his stun rifle. Shorty got his gun ready almost at the same time. The others took a few seconds to catch up.

"Don't fucking move unless you *really* want to piss yourself, bitches," Trey shouted. "And, yeah, Howard, I think you should give a shit that we're from the Brownstone Agency. You come with us all nice and quiet like, and we don't have to do this the hard way. Otherwise, lots of pain gonna come to you and yours."

Howard glared at Trey and thrust his hand out. "Kill those motherfuckers."

The Bay Boys all pulled out their guns, but no one fired. The gang members frowned and exchanged looks.

"I told you to kill those motherfuckers!" Howard thundered.

Trey clucked his tongue. "See, they all don't want to open fire and bust up these nice motherfucking wheels. I can't blame them. They are sweet rides."

Howard gritted his teeth. "If you don't kill those motherfuckers, I'll kill you."

A Bay Boy pulled the trigger. His bullet shattered the windshield of the purple monstrosity.

"Damn," Trey shouted. "Now you've gone and done it."

He put two blue bolts into the man and the twitching criminal fell to the ground.

Hostilities now exchanged, everyone opened up. The bounty hunters rolled behind several of the cars, spinning around to take a few quick shots, sending blue stun bolts toward the criminals. The gang members stood in a rough line, pelting their own vehicles with bullet after bullet and ignoring the cries of their men as they went down twitching and drooling.

Got to give them points for discipline.

Isaiah jerked back as a bullet struck his shoulder. Deshawn pulled him behind a car and applied pressure to the wound.

Trey frowned.

The Bay Boys started to advance, and he popped up to fire a few quick shots. Shorty joined him, then screamed and fell to the ground.

"Motherfucker," Shorty yelled, clutching his crotch. "That motherfucker shot me in the balls. I still need those!"

Trey blasted a gang member right between the eyes with a stun bolt. The man wet himself as he fell.

"Isaiah and Shorty, drink your damned potions before you bleed out, you dumbass bitches," Trey shouted.

His jaw clenched, Shorty yanked out his potion and downed it in one gulp. Deshawn helped Isaiah. Within thirty seconds, both men were breathing normally.

Trey frowned and looked at his rifle; only thirty percent power left. He'd need to change out the power cell soon. "This is what we get for not just mowing all their asses down with our real guns." He rolled behind another vehicle, squeezing off a few shots in between.

Two of the gang members fell, struck in the chests. Trey realized he had no idea what it'd take to stop a stun rifle shot. They did have a relatively short effective range, one of the reasons even most police departments didn't use them.

Trey hissed in pain as a bullet slammed into his chest. It didn't pierce the vest, but the throbbing ache felt almost like he'd busted a rib.

I fucking hate *getting shot.*

"Get ready for the rainy day, boys," Trey called.

He ducked around the car and emptied his power cell with a flurry of wild shots. The rest of the bounty hunters took advantage of the suppressive fire to aim their shots at the gang members who were closing on them. Just a couple of minutes after the fight had started it was over, twitching and drooling gang members strewn about the courtyard.

Trey slapped a new energy cell into the stun rifle and patted the bullet-riddled car next to him. "This shit needed a new look anyway." He glanced at the others. "Anyone else get a free vasectomy?"

Max and Deshawn snorted.

Shorty glanced down at his bloody pants. "Shit. I'm healed, but do you realize how bad getting shot in the nuts hurts?" He reached down and groped himself. "I'm afraid if I don't keep checkin', I'll find out they're gone."

Trey rolled his eyes. "Stop your bitching. A lot of money was spent to save your balls. Yo, Isaiah, you all right?"

Isaiah nodded and moved his arm in a circle, testing it. "Yeah. Shit, never done this magic potion stuff before. It's like I didn't get shot at all."

"This shit was sloppy as fuck, even if we were using non-lethals." Trey kicked the tire of the nearest vehicle, but it was already flat from being a bullet-sponge. "But at least they're all out, and you men still have your dicks. Go zip-tie all their asses."

Trey jogged over toward the white-suited bounty. The man was still breathing, though he was bleeding from a gunshot wound to the leg. His gun lay several yards away, and he glared up at Trey, obviously not stunned.

The bounty hunter laughed. "This is too damned perfect. Your dumbass gang assholes shot you in the cross-fire?" Trey nodded and rubbed his chin. "Deshawn, go to Lachlan and get the first aid kit. We'll patch this bastard up and call for an ambulance."

Deshawn nodded and jogged away.

Trey smiled down at Howard. "You're damned lucky. It could have been a lot worse. Told you you should have just come with us."

Howard winced. "Lucky?" he rasped. "I got fucking *shot*. How could it have been worse?"

Trey shrugged. "At least you didn't get shot in the balls."

15

James parked the rental SUV several blocks from the target house. He'd learned this lesson the hard way the previous day when they'd flown to Utah to check out a Council safe house. Sure, they'd kicked down the doors and taken out the flunkies inside, and they'd even scored a few minor artifacts in addition to one of the artifacts missing from the museum, but that didn't change the fact that a fireball had reduced their SUV to a smoking ruin.

Senator Johnston had been very obliging about sending a helicopter for them, but it was still embarrassing as fuck, and even with all the money James had, he didn't like spending it on replacing rental SUVs.

James grunted and looked at Shay in the passenger seat. "They might have already cleared out. Maybe we should have hit these places simultaneously."

She smiled and slapped a magazine into her pistol. She holstered it and then started loading shells into her shotgun. "I don't think we're ready for that yet, not until

Dannec delivers the anti-magic deflectors. You and I might be used to dealing with high-level magic shit, but not your guys, and it's not like the Council will clear out of every possible safehouse in the United States just because we hit one."

"True enough."

James opened the door and stepped out, tugging on the ugly gray coat that concealed his tactical holster and array of weapons. Shay attached a strap to the shotgun and slung it over her shoulder. She grabbed her *tachi* scabbard out of the back seat. Subtlety wasn't part of her strategy on this raid.

Shay sighed. "And please tell me you already informed the cops that you were raiding this place and they should stay the fuck away."

"The cops in Utah left pretty quickly once we explained."

"Yeah, because I *so* loved having forty guns pointed at me." Shay rolled her eyes. "I don't want to have to explain to another bunch of cops why I'm a walking arsenal."

James nodded. "Yeah. They know. I've asked the Vegas cops to stay clear through my local police contacts, but they have people on the way to patrol the perimeter. They've been making calls to nearby houses to tell people to shelter in place, and as long as we keep the damage to the safe house, it shouldn't be a big deal. Maybe I'll spread a little cash around as an apology if I do some damage."

Shay laughed. "Look at you. You're turning into a big softy."

He grunted. "Just trying to make sure I only piss off

people who deserve it. That way I have less to confess when I go to church."

Shay grinned. "I'll try not to burn down the block." She winked. "Don't worry. I'll dip into my own funds if I cause any collateral damage." She patted the shotgun. "Great anti-personnel damage, low on penetration. Perfect raid weapon."

He shrugged. "Shit happens. Just don't get killed."

"If I even get seriously wounded, I will be surprised."

The pair marched down the street toward the subdued suburban ranch house. The perfectly manicured lawn with a single palm tree and a white picket fence made it look like a slice of normal southwestern living rather than a safe house for a dangerous multi-planetary criminal cabal.

Guess I can't just blow the whole thing up. Bad idea anyway, since there might be a few artifacts inside. This shit's easier when they don't hide in the suburbs.

Shay glanced at James. "You bonded yet?"

He shook his head. "Might as well get it over with."

James took a deep breath and reached under his shirt. He pulled the separator off the back of the amulet and let it touch his chest. He hissed as tendrils shot into his body. His coat and shirt would conceal the truth from anyone spying, eye or drone, but they might wonder about his gritted teeth.

Initiation, the amulet broadcast into his mind. *Insufficient power for advanced transformation. Increase power to kill enemies more efficiently.*

The chattier and more understandable Whispy Doom had grown in the past few months, the more their mental discussions seemed to center around the amulet trying to persuade James in increasingly elaborate ways to get pissier and more violent. Not something he needed a lot of help with.

These assholes won't need the full suit from what I've seen.

Find stronger enemies. Adapt and become stronger.

You're like the fucking wrestling coach from hell.

Find stronger enemies. Kill. Adapt and become stronger.

James snorted and moved toward the fence. He nodded to Shay. "You want front or back this time?"

Shay ran her tongue along the inside of her cheek. "I'll take back. The more interesting guys ran out back last time."

"Do you have your magic shield?"

She raised a hand to reveal a small iron ring inlaid with intricate symbols. "Yes, Dad," she retorted sarcastically.

"Okay. I'll give you a minute to get into place."

Shay gave him a mock salute and jogged past the side fence, disappearing around the back. James advanced toward the front gate and just stood staring at the house. The enemy had probably already seen him, and he hoped they had. Unless one of the Council members were actually in the house, he doubted the fight would last long.

Find Council. Find stronger enemies. Kill. Adapt and become stronger.

Yeah. Yeah. I know, Coach Doom. Challenge myself until I'm the best. Pain is just weakness leaving the body and all that shit.

"Coach" is incorrect designation.

James chuckled. *What, you like Whispy Doom more?*

The amulet didn't answer, and the bounty hunter grinned. That was the first time he'd even gotten the amulet to shut up using a thought rather than an action.

"Ah, fuck it." James hopped the fence and pulled out his .45. He advanced toward the front door, waiting for a fireball, lightning blast, or bullets. Nothing came.

He glanced at the house number to verify the address. The last thing he wanted to do was bash in the door and scare some innocent old lady.

This is the right place. These guys aren't nearly as proactive as their buddies in Utah. That should have been enough time for Shay to get to the back. One...two...three...

James smashed his boot into the front door. It sailed off its hinges and flew several yards until crashing into a couch.

Four men inside the living room opened fire with assault rifles. The bounty hunter clenched his jaw as bullet after bullet struck him and bounced off, falling to the floor. The shots stung but didn't accomplish much more than adding not-so-fashionable holes to his coat and shirt.

He raised his .45 and lined up the first gunmen's head. He waited a few seconds as they pelted him with bullets, the frustration growing on their faces.

They actually thought that shit would work.

A bullet ripped into the door frame, blasting wood and dust over his face.

Fuck, better finish this before they end up shooting someone across the street.

One of the gunmen swallowed, his eyes widening.

"Wondering why I'm not dying?" James asked. He shot the man. "People keep trying, but it just doesn't take. My girlfriend says I'm pretty stubborn."

The other three turned to run, and he nailed two and

missed the third. The poor bastard threw open the kitchen door, only to find Shay holding a shotgun.

She smiled. "Hello and goodbye."

Buckshot shredded the man, and his blood splattered all over the couch.

"Is anyone from the fucking *Council* here?" James shouted. "Or is it nothing but fucking cannon-fodder assholes?"

A bedroom door opened, and a muscular man stepped out. He growled several times and pounded his fists together, and an orange aura oozed from his skin and surrounded him.

James and Shay exchanged looks, and both fired. The bullets and pellets bounced off the new arrival.

Shay frowned. "That's some annoying shit."

With a roar, the man charged. James tossed his pistol to the side and rushed forward to meet the enemy. He tackled the man, bringing him to the ground, but his opponent smashed a fist into the side of the bounty hunter's head. The force of the blow sent James into a nearby wall, his large body leaving an equally large hole.

Huh. So that's *what it feels like.*

Shay fired another shotgun blast, but Mr. Muscles didn't even flinch. He pushed himself to his feet and glared at James.

Kill, Whispy Doom commanded. *No new adaptations from enemy. Eliminate and find stronger enemies and new sources of adaptations.*

Yeah, yeah. I'm not gonna let him feel like a big man for too long, Coach Doom.

The bounty hunter extricated himself from the wall and

cracked his knuckles. "You got in one good hit, I'll give you that, asshole. Now it's my turn."

James rushed toward the man and threw his punch. The man blocked it but wasn't prepared for the bounty hunter's knee. He grimaced and stumbled back. They traded blows, but neither got more than a grunt out of the other.

Insufficient power for advanced transformation. Increase power to kill enemy more efficiently.

Shut the fuck up. I don't need your blade or extra armor to finish this asshole.

James threw an elbow toward the man's throat. Mr. Muscles took it with a hiss but didn't go down. He stopped and checked the man's face. No blood. It wouldn't be a simple matter of shoving his gun or blade in his mouth.

His enemy pounded his fists together again, and his aura grew brighter.

Shay rolled her eyes. "This is painful to watch. You might as well just whip out your dick and see who can pee farther." She pulled out her sword and tossed it hilt-first to James. "Finish his ass already. This obviously isn't one of their main bases, and this meathead isn't going to know anything important."

James snatched the sword out of the air. "This is a Masamune *tachi*. I doubt you can take it. Last chance to surrender."

Mr. Muscles raised his hand and gestured for James to attack.

He shrugged. "Your funeral."

The bounty hunter charged the man, keeping the sword level. His enemy smirked, confident in his invulnerability. A few seconds after James had run him through, the smirk faded and panic registered on his face. James pulled the sword out and stabbed the man a few more times before stepping back and holding the weapon out to Shay.

Mr. Muscles fell to the ground face-first, a pool of his own blood already spreading beneath him. He took a few shuddering breaths and died, and the orange glow faded.

She sheathed the blade after wiping it off on one of the dead men's shirts. "Should have rubbed two brain cells together. What kind of idiot sees someone pull out a sword in this day and age and doesn't assume it's magical?"

James grunted.

I didn't know it'd work against me the first time.

The damned amulet laughed at him. He was sure of it.

Find stronger enemies. Adapt and become stronger.

Shay tilted her head and pointed to the dead man. "Check out his ears."

James looked down at the corpse. The man was wearing jade earrings.

"What? You jealous of his fashion sense?"

Shay laughed. "No, the Professor's list. Those things have way higher limits than that guy was showing. With a proper magical infusion, he could have kicked you half-way across the county."

"Oh, yeah." James knelt and yanked out the earrings, slipping them into a pouch. "This shit is gonna get annoying if we're going to have to go house to house and kill a half-dozen guys at a time."

"Peyton and Heather are working on it." She shrugged. "Besides, the more we take out, the fewer places they have to hide. From Johnston's info, they've lost a lot of guys already. They might purposely be trying to spread themselves out to avoid a single decisive strike."

James grunted. "I don't give a shit about the flunkies. We take out Council members, the rest won't know what to do." He grimaced. "I guess we'll just have to keep smoking them out until they crawl out of their holes."

He glared down at the body. Whispy Doom was right. He wanted stronger enemies.

Yes, the amulet hissed. *Find stronger enemies. Kill them. Adapt and become stronger.*

16

Tyler stared at a smiling blond man in the corner chatting up a young woman. Kathy kept shooting glares at the Casanova, but he didn't seem to notice.

Stone Hanson. How many girls have you sold off to twisted sons of bitches?

She walked over to Tyler and leaned over to whisper. "You telling me your neutrality extends to that trafficking trash?"

The bartender shrugged. "Extends to everyone. I don't call the cops on murderers who come in here."

"Killing a person's spirit is almost worse than murdering them," the brunette snapped. "And it's not like neutrality means you have to let everyone in here, just that you don't call the cops."

Tyler rubbed his chin. "You have a good point. You think you can watch the bar for a while? I'm going to go take Mr. Hanson to meet someone."

Kathy smirked. "Brownstone?"

"Nope. Someone just as interesting, though."

"I've got the bar." She nodded toward Hanson. "You take care of him."

Tyler smiled as he pulled up the hinge and stepped out from behind the bar. "Oh, don't worry about it. I've got someone very interested in meeting him."

He headed straight toward Hanson's table and smiled down at the woman. "Leave. I need to talk with him."

The woman frowned and rolled her eyes. "Whatever." She smiled at Hanson. "Call me, sweetie. I don't give out my number to just anyone."

Hanson gave her a smile featuring gleaming white teeth. He maintained the smile until she was out of the bar. The second the door closed, he glared at Tyler.

The bartender sat down across from him. "Problem?"

"What the fuck was that about?" Hanson nodded toward the door. "You're messing with my night."

Tyler leaned forward and plastered a smile on his face. "You're a businessman. I'm a businessman. I have a business opportunity that requires a man of your...skill set, but it's kind of a limited-time thing, so I didn't want to waste time while you hit on some bimbo."

Hanson's frown faded. "Okay, I'm willing to get involved, but if I'm doing the legwork, I want a seventy-thirty split. That's not up for negotiation."

Tyler shrugged. "Sounds fair to me. You got time right now? There's someone I want you to meet."

Hanson nodded. "Yeah. Lead on."

A half-hour later, Tyler and Hanson stood in the Eyes' dark and smoky room.

Hanson frowned. "What the fuck is this shit?" He pointed at the Eyes. "I've heard of you, some freaky Oriceran information broker, and you like mindfuck people, but they get off on it. Better than dust."

"Yes," the Eyes hissed. "Better than dust. Oh, so rapturous."

Hanson nodded, and a smile slowly formed on his face. "Wait. You mindfuck some of these people, and they're not dead from what I saw walking in here." He snapped. "You want to establish a new revenue stream. You need someone to offload the merchandise." He patted his chest. "I'm your man. I can get them out of the city or the country. I've got clients all over, firmly established and guarded distribution routes, and partners. Now, some of my more exclusive clients have specific tastes, but I can unload anyone. It'll just be you'll earn more cash for some than the others."

Tyler managed not to gag, either at Hanson or concerning what was likely about to happen to him.

"Perfect," the Eyes wheezed.

Hanson grinned and slapped Tyler on the arm. "Yeah, this is great. I'll give you a little bonus for hooking me up—"

The trafficker's eyes rolled up in the back of his head, and he collapsed to the ground drooling. Light bands flowed up and down his body.

Tyler looked down at Hanson. "What are you going to do with him?"

"An experiment. I need to test the limits." The Eyes let out a quiet laugh.

"The limits of what?"

"Of the human mind and its tolerance of pain."

Tyler winced and swallowed. "Okay, so I gave you what you needed. Now, don't you owe me some information? And not generic fortune-teller shit."

He stuck his hands behind his back so the Eyes wouldn't see him trembling.

The Eyes disappeared entirely, and when he spoke next, his voice seemed to come from all around the room.

"The Council. They aren't what you think. No grand plans of conquest. No purity of ideology. This isn't magic over technology, or Oriceran over Earth. No, no, no. Nothing like that at all. Far, far from it."

Tyler surveyed the room slowly, not liking having nothing to focus on other than the unconscious and drooling man at his feet. "If they aren't interested in that sort of crap, then why gather an army? Why stockpile dangerous artifacts?"

The Eyes chuckled. "You of all people should understand that there is another use for strength than conquering."

"I make a living using my brain, not my muscles. I'm not Brownstone."

"Yes…Brownstone."

Yellow eyes reappeared a few inches above Hanson's body.

Tyler couldn't stop himself from jumping back.

This guy is creepy as fuck. Did he escape from some Oriceran mental hospital?

He took a few deep breaths. "What about Brownstone?"

"He's strong," the Eyes replied. "Strong enough that he

could have seized wealth by taking it. Instead, he let the followers of the Resurrected God warp him, turn him into a defender. He punishes the darkness to earn his money, praying to his Lord to forgive his sins, even though he could make his own law with his power."

Tyler snorted. "That's your great insight? That Brownstone isn't a complete asshole because he was raised by priests? I already knew that shit."

"I use him as an example." The Eyes drifted into a corner. "The Council has great power. There are six. No. I hear there are four now left. All powerful in their own ways. Crazak, a most ambitious Light Elf. Yilin, an Eastern Frostling, mistress of ice magic. Ferrao, a gnome of exquisite and diabolical ability when it comes to dark artifacts, and He Who Hunts."

Tyler laughed. "'He Who Hunts?' What kind of fucked up name is that?"

"Even I don't know what he is, and I don't think they do either. A summoned being, perhaps a creation of dark magics long forgotten. He lives to kill and seeks chaos. It's odd, really." The Eyes chuckled. "The Council doesn't seek chaos, but he does. Their goals aren't compatible."

"What does the Council want, then?"

"The same as anyone. The same as you."

Tyler blinked, and his eyes widened. "Just power and influence? That's it? No supervillain plans to take over the Earth and become new royalty or some shit?"

"Yes," the Eyes hissed. "Nothing more. Nothing less. Ruling is difficult. Why do people rule? For power. For wealth. Skip the ruling and just go for the power and wealth. Find the opportunities and exploit them. That's what the Council believes."

"I don't get it. You're saying they're just a bunch of businessmen?" Tyler furrowed his brow.

"No. Like you and me, they're more interested in the more efficient collection of power and wealth. Criminals who seek to take advantage of a great opportunity, Earth, a place that had been all but stripped of its true magic for millennia. They moved slowly and subtly, gathered their time and resources, their contacts. A senator, a minister of parliament. If they'd waited long enough, maybe even a president or prime minister." The Eyes wheezed. "But they pushed too hard and too fast. They chose the wrong city with the wrong defender. Decades of effort, now on the precipice. Perhaps wasted, but they aren't done. Each individual Council member has tremendous magical ability, and they've collected artifacts. They intended to research them and copy them. To create servants who would be too powerful for most to challenge, while sitting in the shadows and pulling the strings. Control without rule."

Tyler blinked several times and stared at the darkened wall. All of this meant that if Brownstone hadn't gotten involved, the Council might have gotten away with all their artifacts and no one would have even known to start looking into them. Hell, for that matter, Tyler had played his part.

Did I help save the fucking world from some super-Oriceran mafia?

A broad grin struck his face.

"Too hard," the Eyes whispered. "Too hard and too fast. Balance. Equilibrium. Let the light push the darkness back, and then let it return. Those without subtlety deserve no subtle treatment. I will reward you, Tyler, for services rendered past and present. I've heard things. I know you are striking at them, but you're only striking at fingers. It's time to cut off some limbs."

Tyler smacked a fist into his palm. "We're tracking those bastards down, and we're taking them out."

His phone buzzed with a text.

"Look at it," the Eyes insisted.

Tyler looked down at the phone. Three sets of two numbers, each separated by a comma.

"What are these?"

"Enough to restore balance." The Eyes disappeared. "Now leave me. I have to begin my experiments." A quiet giggle followed.

Tyler glanced down at the unconscious Hanson one last time before opening the door and stepping outside. He gave a nod to the two guards and headed down the hallway, doing his best to ignore all the blissed-out people in the building.

He forwarded the text to the contact numbers he'd been given for Heather and Peyton.

> **I got this from a contact. I have no fucking idea what it means. Maybe you can make heads or tails of it.**

The next afternoon, James threw a laminated picture on the table in the briefing room. Shay, Lieutenant Hall, Tyler, and Trey all leaned in to peer at it. It was a map of the United States, with three locations circled, one in Colorado, another in Northern California, and a third in West Texas.

Trey chuckled. "Planning your next few vacations, big man?"

James grunted. "If I go on vacation, I'll probably end up having to kill some ancient monster that just woke up."

Tyler arched an eyebrow. "They figured it out? They know what those numbers meant."

James grunted. "Coordinates, once you spread the numbers out. Longitude and latitude. How did you get this shit?"

The information broker shook his head. "Trust me, you don't want to know. I don't even want to remember."

Trey smirked, but James didn't know what was going through his head.

Shay pointed at the map. "So the Council members are there?"

James shrugged. "Maybe. I thought about asking Johnston for help, but that might end up leaking to the Council. We need to be careful and gather as much information as we can so we don't make the same mistakes as the government, and I think the best way to handle that is the old-fashioned way. No funny magic or satellites or shit."

Lieutenant Hall frowned. "Meaning what? What old-fashioned way?"

He pointed at the map. "Meaning something you cops love. A stakeout. Dannec sent me a message this morning, he's ready to deliver most of what I need. We can equip some teams and stake out the locations. Just for observation, but at least we know they won't be defenseless. If we verify the Council members are there, then we send everyone there. All the locations are within an hour by supersonic flight."

She nodded. "I think I'm going to take a little time off to help you with this. It's like you said—I'm a cop, and we're good at stakeouts."

James nodded. "Fine, then. I'll lead a team with a few guys. Trey will lead some guys. And you and Shay can be a team. We'll watch these fuckers for a few days and see if we spot any roaches that need to be squashed."

He grunted and stared down at the map. With each base or safehouse that fell, the Council had fewer places to hide. The noose was tightening.

You fuckers should have run all the way back to Oriceran if you didn't want me coming after you.

17

James grunted as he looked through his binoculars at the mountain cabin. No activity. Sitting in a fucking truck for days was torture, especially since the men he had with him were rigid as statues half the time: Lachlan, Deshawn, and Max. The worst part was he was in a damned Chevy. The rental place had been out of Fords, but at least the thing was big enough that it wasn't cramped for four grown men.

I know I don't exactly hang out with them all the time, but it's not like I'm gonna fucking put them through a wall if they look at me the wrong way. Shit, not even a wall for hundreds of feet to put them through.

He chuckled.

"You see something, Mr. Brownstone?" asked Lachlan from the front passenger seat.

"Same shit as before, just some cabins. No one's up there, not that I can see."

"Maybe Tyler's info was shit." Lachlan frowned.

Deshawn snored, his head resting against the back

window and drooling. He'd taken most of the night shift along with Max. The other man snored on the other side, but he managed not to drool.

James grunted. "Maybe. I wish the fucking Council would hurry and show up so we could kick their asses already. Fucking pussies."

Lachlan grinned. "Yeah." He laughed. "It's funny."

"What is?"

"I mean you're a class-six bounty hunter, the Scourge of Motherfucking Harriken, the Granite Ghost, but you're just like us. You don't want to sit around on your hands. You want to beat the asses of those dumbass motherfuckers."

James shrugged. "I don't mind relaxing, but when it's time to do a job, I like to get it over with. I became a bounty hunter because I'm tough, and it was a good way to make money while cleaning up trash. I don't have to worry about a bunch of paperwork and evidence shit like cops do."

Lachlan laughed. "I hear that, big man."

Good. At least one of them is finally loosening up.

The young man's smile disappeared, and he looked down at his hands. "Shit."

James frowned. "What?"

"I'm sorry."

"For what?"

Lachlan sighed. "The first time I ever seen you, you were in your truck. I wanted to jack your fine-ass wheels."

"Everyone with brains appreciates a classic Ford." James chuckled. "Good thing you didn't. That would have ended badly and painfully for you."

The younger bounty hunter snorted. "Yeah, I didn't get that far. I told Trey I wanted to do that, and he laid into me about respect and showed me a video of you kicking ass." He shook his head. "But then you got all those guys to quit the gang and go join up with you, and I thought they were pussies at first. So I was a dumbass again." He shrugged. "Now I have a good job, and even the 5-0 respect me. The way I was going before, I would have been dead in a few years. Now I got some shit to look forward to, and it's all because of you."

James shook his head. "I haven't done jack. Royce was the one that whipped you guys into shape. Trey and the other guys were the ones who gave you the real second chance. I'm just a guy who is good at kicking ass, and needed some help to kick more."

Lachlan grinned. "Just saying, big man—you could have been one of those high-level guys you hunt. You could have busted up banks like King Pyro or killed like that crazy bitch at the farmer's market. But you ain't doing that, even though everyone knows you're the baddest motherfucker in America."

When James activated Whispy Doom, the amulet constantly stressed killing and defeating his enemies. He didn't need to be a xenopsychologist to understand that his home planet must be filled with violent, warlike assholes.

Then again, I'm a violent asshole half the time.

"Some priests gave a damn when I was young," James explained. "They taught me about right and wrong. Taught me that no matter how powerful someone thinks they are, there's always a more powerful being watching you and that it's the duty of the strong to protect the weak." He shrugged.

"I'm not perfect, and I've fucked up a lot in my life, but the one thing I've realized this last year is that I'm a part of the world, not some fucking island, and I owe a little something to it. I'll never be as good as the men who raised me, but if I can fight against the kind of people I might have been and make money on the side, well, why wouldn't I do that?"

Lachlan stared at him and nodded slowly. "Damn, big man. I ain't ever knew you was so deep. That's some Marcus Aurelius shit right there."

James grunted. "Deep as a puddle."

Lachlan grinned and shifted to look at the cabin, bringing up his own binoculars. "How long we gonna sit here and stare at this empty bullshit?"

"Until I get bored."

"How long is that gonna take?"

James chuckled. "No barbeque out here, so not long."

Shay tapped the side of her AR goggles. "Magnify 10x. Activate Thermal Mode One."

She moved her head slowly as she surveyed the sprawling mansion in the distance. A few small thermal signatures here and there, but all obviously animals. Nothing looked humanoid, or even non-humanoid and Oriceran.

Maria peered through her decidedly-less-sexy binoculars. "Now I remember why I joined AET. So much of investigation is boring, and now I'm using my vacation time to sit around on a stakeout." She snickered.

Shay laughed. "When I'm working on tomb raids, I'm as excited by the research beforehand as I am by the actual raid. In another life, I might have ended up as a regular archaeologist." She tapped her goggles to deactivate the enhanced mode and pushed them up her head.

She pulled out her phone to cycle through some of the drone feeds.

"Think they might spot them?" Maria asked. She lowered her binoculars.

The tomb raider shrugged. "Maybe, but I'd rather not stare at them for a while. Peyton's got a bunch of algos set up to send me a message if there's unusual activity, so it's not even like I have to do much. Heather's got decent coverage at the other sites, although magical types have a way of hiding from machines, so it's still good we're here in person."

Maria whistled. "All this fancy tech. I meant to ask the other day, why isn't Brownstone using it, or his guys? I mean, I know his hacker has got her eyes in the sky, but why not the fancy AR goggles and shit like that?"

Shay laughed. "Because James clings to the delusion that he can maintain a simple life despite being a class-six bounty hunter with a half-Drow adopted daughter and a tomb-raider girlfriend. He doesn't like fancy tech, and by extension, his agency doesn't like fancy tech, except for the occasional jammer." She grinned. "I, however, believe in working smarter, not harder."

The cop sighed and leaned back in her seat. "If you went back in time and just picked what you wanted to do, what would it have been? I mean, I know life pushes us in directions, but say you knew everything you knew now. Would you be the regular archaeologist after all?"

Shay furrowed her brow for a moment, then pulled the AR goggles off her head and set them on the car's console. "Anything?"

"Yeah? Anything."

"Yeah, I guess I would be a professor." Shay shrugged. "I already give lectures, you know, on history and archaeology."

Maria blinked. "How did you swing that? You don't strike me as the type who spent years in school earning her Ph.D."

"According to my official records, I did." Shay chuckled. "I love history and archaeology. I have for a long time. Love that we were so wrong about it. We thought we knew what was up, but we knew shit. When I see some of these students…" She sighed. "It's weird. They think they're worldly, but they're so innocent. Even Alison isn't as innocent as some of these kids, but then again, she's dealt with a lot of darkness."

"So it annoys you, then? That they're clueless?"

Shay shook her head. "No, because they still bring themselves to give a fuck about quaint shit like, 'What is truth?' and 'What actually happened in the past?' instead of just, 'How can I make the most money?'"

Maria nodded, bringing up her binoculars again. "I think about career crap a lot lately. I was even joking about it with Sergeant Weber before telling him I was taking some time off. I became a cop to help people, but half the time anymore I wonder. City Hall's more interested in looking good than protecting people. It's like they aren't happy unless I'm reporting the same shit six different ways and writing memos telling people how to wipe their asses."

Shay snickered. "I wouldn't know. I've never worked for anyone. Sure, I've had many clients, but they don't tell me what to do, just what they want."

The cop chuckled and shook her head. She looked out the window for a long moment before turning back toward Shay. "Can I ask you a personal question? You can tell me to fuck off if you don't want to answer."

"Need to know the question before I can tell you to fuck off."

"Before all this, you weren't exactly a tomb raider."

Shay snorted. "That's not a question, and you already know the answer."

Maria lowered the binoculars and locked eyes with Shay. "Yeah, but what I don't get is why. You're damned smart, and you just told me how much you would have liked to have gone into being a professor." She frowned. "Look, I've been a cop for a long time. Too long. It's hard for me to remember at times that the average person isn't a piece-of-shit criminal. Being in AET is even worse because I run into all these people with extraordinary abilities who use them to be even bigger pieces of shit. You're...unusual."

"I don't have any special powers."

"But you were still one of the top hitmen in the game, and you managed to disappear when half the world was looking for you." Maria took a deep breath. "And not only that, you walked away, which means on some level you weren't a hitman because you got off on killing people."

Shay looked to the side. "Maybe. I don't know. I've got a sob story about how I got into it, but I'm sure everyone does. Also not gonna lie and pretend I didn't get excited by a well-executed hit, but it wears on you, and after a while, I got tired of thinking I was going to end up dead in a pool of my own blood, shot in the face by someone I thought was a friend. So I ended that life and started a new one. It has taken me a while to actually turn into someone other than the killer, but here I am—Shay Carson, tomb raider. Don't know if I'm a better or worse person, but I'm sure as hell different."

Maria nodded, a thoughtful expression on her face. "Thanks for telling me. You really didn't have to."

Shay shrugged, then grinned. "Need something to fill the time."

Trey stared through the binoculars at the house and barn in the distance and snorted. Nothing but cows wandering the fenced fields and chewing their cud. Same as always. The bounty hunters were hidden in an abandoned barn a half-mile away. No people, nasty smell, but nice view of the target site.

I never thought being a bounty hunter would mean I'd have to sit and stare at cows.

He glanced at the SUV. Shorty was looking at his phone and eating candy. Manuel was nodding to himself, singing along to some song only he could hear through his earbuds. Isaiah and Russell were sleeping. The poor bastards had had the night shift.

Shorty opened the door, then stepped out and popped a Milk Dud into his mouth. He chewed it for a few seconds and swallowed before saying, "You see any magical bitches yet, or is it gonna be as boring as yesterday? I was thinkin' the most boring thing in the world is watchin' grass grow, but nah. The most boring thing is watchin' grass grow, and cows eat it."

"Nope. Still just seeing a lot of cows. I can't believe no all-powerful evil magical dudes are gonna hang out at a ranch around cows. Shouldn't they have a sweet-ass castle or tower or some shit?" Trey snorted. "I think we got bad info from Tyler."

Manuel opened his door and stepped out. He pulled out his earbuds. "How do you know it's not a trick?"

Trey turned to look at him, not sure if he'd heard the previous conversation. "A trick?"

"Yeah. It's magic, right? So the fuckers use it to disguise themselves as cows, or maybe you have to run at the barn with a tractor to go through the magical portal or something like that."

Trey chuckled. "Maybe. You never know with this shit."

Shorty downed another Milk Dud, his eyes narrowing. "You know, I have a cousin who lives in Oklahoma. His dad had a small ranch." He frowned and shook his head. "Cows are fuckin' valuable, man. No wonder people used to jack them back in the day." He nodded toward the ranch. "Now imagine you had some sweet-ass wheels, right? But a lot of them. Would you just park them somewhere and let them sit and never check on them?"

Trey blinked. "What the fu— Shit." His eyes widened.

Shortly nodded. "Exactly."

Manuel looked between the two of them. "What?"

Trey grinned at Manuel. "You're right."

"I'm right about what?"

"It being a trick. We just ain't thought of it before because we're a bunch of city boys who ain't used to looking at ranches." He pointed toward the ranch. "We ain't seen no actual human over there since we got there. Yeah, cows eat grass and shit, but there still should be someone checking on things."

He pulled out his phone. "I'm gonna call the big man. I think it's time for at least a quick look inside. Ain't no one home to complain if we inspect their house."

Trey, Shorty, Manuel, and Isaiah rushed toward the fence line under cover of darkness. There was nowhere to really hide, so they didn't even bother, although dark suits and dark tactical harnesses helped them blend into the shadows, with the help of the cloudy night. The four men, suited and with anti-magic deflectors around their necks, vaulted over the low wooden fence.

So far, so good. No murderous wizard bitches.

James had okayed them taking a closer look, but wanted them to pull out immediately if they encountered any resistance.

Trey took point as they rushed down the long dirt road leading from the main road to the front of the actual home. It looked modest now, almost smaller than the nearby barn. They'd not seen any movement or light from it in days, and that trend continued.

"Yo, Trey," Shorty whispered. "Have you thought about what we gonna do if the 5-0 show up?"

"We surrender immediately, and we tell them to call the big man. Simple as shit, but I don't think no 5-0 are gonna show up. The Council bitches picked this place for a reason. We're in the middle of Bumfuck Nowhere, Texas, and I ain't seen no cops. No sheriff, no highway patrol. We ain't barely seen any cars. No fucking cops are gonna show up in the middle of the night all of a sudden."

They arrived at the front door.

Shorty pointed away from the house. "Look."

Trey turned to look. The cows were gone. "Motherfucking illusions." He nodded to Manuel. "Do your thing, brother." He pulled out a small flashlight and shined it on the lock.

The other man fished out a small pouch containing lockpicking tools. "It's been a while. Usually, y'all just kick the door down or shoot it."

"It gets the job done." Trey smirked.

Shorty and Isaiah moved to either side of the porch, their guns out, scanning the inky darkness for enemies.

A half-minute later, the front door clicked, and Manuel grinned.

"Everyone get out their flashlights," Trey ordered.

They all complied, holding their flashlights with their left hands and setting their right arms atop their left to stabilize their shooting arms.

Trey nodded. "Three...two...one."

He threw open the door and rushed in, sweeping the area with his light. The only enemy he encountered was dust. The other men rushed in, weapons ready.

Trey flipped on a light switch, half-expecting some

hideous ghoul to appear, not just a slightly dated living room set with a really unfortunate orange color scheme.

"Watch the door, Isaiah. Manuel, you back him up. Shorty, you're with me."

The men all nodded their acknowledgment.

Trey and Shorty hit the kitchen, bathroom, and bedrooms in rapid order. There was no evidence that anyone had been there recently. Even the refrigerator was empty, and the beds lacked sheets or blankets.

The bounty hunters made their way to the back door and searched the area off the back porch with their flashlights.

"Hey," Shorty whispered, "you see that?" He pointed with his flashlight.

Trey narrowed his eyes at a bump in the distance. "What the fuck is that?"

His partner laughed. "What? You ain't never gone nowhere but LA or Vegas, have you? It's a storm cellar. For tornadoes and shit."

"Nice." Trey nodded. "Go get the guys. We're gonna poke inside and see if someone's worried about a storm named Brownstone coming."

Shorty nodded and rushed off. Fifteen seconds later, all three men returned.

Trey grinned and rushed outside. The other men fell in behind him in an inverted wedge formation. The team sprinted toward the storm cellar and surrounded it, their weapons pointed down.

"On three," Trey whispered. He knelt by the huge wooden door and held up a finger, then two, then three. He grabbed the door and felt no resistance. It was unlocked.

He threw it open.

A long hiss pierced the still night. Two pairs of slit glowing yellow eyes stared up from the darkened storm cellar. Their flashlights highlighted portions of the massive reptilian creature below, but more importantly, they revealed the ten pairs of legs, each foot tipped with massive claws, and a jaw with three rows of teeth. The monster rushed toward the ladder leading into the cellar.

Trey shot to his feet and backed up. Without even a second of hesitation, he yanked a flashbang from his tactical harness. "Flashbang in." He threw the grenade.

The grenade went off with an echoing pop, and the creature inside let out a huge hiss. When Trey yanked out a frag grenade, the other men followed suit.

"Frag in," they shouted in order, each tossing his grenade. A few seconds later, the explosions rocked the storm cellar. The monster below thrashed and hissed, its blue blood splattering the walls.

"Finish it," Trey shouted. "Conventional rounds first. Keep firing until I tell you otherwise."

The bounty hunters raised their weapons and opened fire, the loud report of their shots echoing in the neighboring space and deafening them.

Trey ran through his magazine. "Cease fire, cease fire!" he shouted.

All three men complied instantly.

Shit. Staff Sergeant's training really is paying off.

Trey chuckled and reloaded his weapon. The other men copied him, and they pointed their flashlights inside the storm cellar. The reptile monster lay dead, dozens of large holes in it. A thin layer of its blood coated the walls and the ground.

"Now that ain't somethin' you see every day," Shorty mumbled. "Even in LA."

Trey chuckled. "Damned right." He pointed with his gun. "Looks like we got ourselves a watchdog, so time to see what it's hiding."

Manuel winced. "You want us to go down in that?"

Shorty smirked. "You want to be workin' for James Brownstone you best remember your balls, no matter what freak-ass monster you're dealin' with." He leapt into the cellar, ignoring the ladder, and landed with a loud thud.

Trey rolled his eyes and shook his head.

"Yo," Shorty called from inside. "You want to see this, Trey. I think it's some magic shit."

Trey slid down the ladder and looked where Shorty's flashlight illuminated the wall.

An intricate pulsing sigil covered the wall.

Shorty frowned. "You think that shit's important?"

Trey lifted his phone to take a picture. "Yup." The air shimmered slightly, and the hairs on the back of his neck stood up. His heart sped up. "Shit. Let's go. Something's wrong."

A low hum filled the cellar.

They exchanged looks and ran for the ladder, scampering out of the storm cellar as the hum grew steadily in volume.

"Run, you sorry bitches," Trey shouted.

The four bounty hunters sprinted away from the storm cellar. A massive explosion erupted, knocking them all to the ground and sending a plume of flame, dirt, and rock into the sky.

Trey winced and rolled over. "Y'all okay?"

Shorty nodded. Manuel groaned and shrugged. Isaiah grunted.

Their leader stood and dusted himself off. He sighed as he felt the back of his suit. There were more than a few new holes.

"I knew I shouldn't have brought a new suit on this motherfucking job."

18

Dannec didn't tense when his alarm spells tripped, though he still grabbed the deadly horn. Just because he was expecting Correk didn't mean he couldn't be ambushed by someone from the Council.

The Fixer stepped through the portal a second later and eyed the horn with a faint smile until the other elf put it away. The portal stayed opened behind him.

Correk held out a thick tome. "This might help in your research. Borrowed from the Library."

Dannec eyed the book for a moment. "They let you check this out?"

"What they don't know," Correk explained, "won't cause me problems later, so please don't spill anything on that." He waved and stepped back through the portal. This time it vanished.

Dannec took the book to a recliner. Trey's discovery of a sigil in the storm cellar had been followed by the other two teams finding different sigils and experiencing equally unpleasant explosions. No one had been injured.

He'd looked at the pictures the teams had sent and had no clue what they meant. He hoped the Fixer's aid would improve the situation. It was obvious from the minimal defenses at the three locations that the Council hadn't anticipated anyone stumbling upon them, and the government's intelligence contained no records of the sites or similar sigils that might shed light on these.

Tyler remained tightlipped about how he'd gotten the information, but Dannec had heard rumors that the Eyes' club had closed down for a few days shortly after Tyler had sent the information to the hackers.

The elf shook his head. Humans sometimes didn't appreciate how dangerous and alien creatures from Oriceran could be.

He opened the tome, which was a rather ancient survey of powerful sigils. From what Correk had told him before his arrival, the book might have dated from before the Great War.

Dannec ran his hand over the page, and the spine glowed. He took a deep breath and imagined the first sigil in his mind. The tome shook and twitched, and he pulled his hand back. The pages began to flip themselves at a furious pace before stopping on a page with the exact sigil he'd envisioned.

He narrowed his eyes as he read. "Interesting. Very interesting."

Just what magic are you playing at, Council?

Tyler stood behind the bar at the Black Sun drinking a beer. James sat on the other side, already on to his second. Shay and Maria chatted quietly at a table in the corner.

The bounty hunter was unsure if his team was making good progress. Dannec was still investigating the sigils they'd found, and they'd recovered a few artifacts, but the main Council members remained hidden, and more importantly, alive. He was frustrated. He'd hoped the bastards would get angry enough to want to come at him. Cat and mouse was not a game he enjoyed.

Tyler took another sip of his beer. "This shit is weird."

James grunted. "Your beer. Your bar."

Tyler chuckled. "No, not that. All this helping you guys take on the Council shit. I've given up on pretending this is about money. There are safer ways to earn money, ones that don't keep me up at night."

"Big money means big danger." The bounty hunter shrugged. He was grateful for Tyler's help, but he wasn't going to sugarcoat the situation.

Time to man up, Tyler.

Tyler sighed. "How do you do it, Brownstone?"

"Do what?"

"Keep going after these assholes." Tyler frowned. "Yeah, I get it, you're a badass, and you have special artifacts and shit, but even you get hurt. Don't you worry that someday you'll go after some bounty and he'll turn out to be tougher than you? That you'll die?"

James gulped down some beer. "Not really."

"Your stones are just that big?"

The bounty hunter shook his head. "Regular cops don't have half the weapons and shit I have. Every time they get a call, they don't know if they're going to go and find some drunk idiot waving around a pellet gun or some demon-summoning witch who's just waiting to kill them because she's bored." James snorted. "Nah. It's not about big balls when you know you're a badass and run toward danger. I'm good at punching shit, so I do."

Tyler nodded slowly. "Yeah. Although AET had access to impressive weapons and equipment, a cop still died going after those Council lackeys. Shit, Maria could have died. I guess I'm just realizing that taking down the Council isn't going to be easy. I thought maybe this shit would be over in a few days."

"Yeah, we need more intel and a bigger hammer." James grunted.

The bartender stared at him like he'd grown a second head.

"What?" James rumbled.

Tyler shrugged. "I always figured your main strategy was to just go in there and beat them down until they lost consciousness."

"That's the simplest strategy, and I like shit simple. But these aren't the kind of people we can just rush at without thinking. We need more information so we can do this shit the smart way. Until then, I'm not going anywhere, and I'm telling everyone else not to go anywhere."

Shay looked over from her table with a grin. "Oh, James Brownstone getting thoughtful. I think I must have been knocked into some parallel universe."

Maria chuckled.

He grunted and shrugged. "Just saying."

The door opened and Dannec stepped through, a smug smile on his face. Everyone turned to look at him.

Tyler frowned. "The door's supposed to be locked."

The elf shrugged. "It was. I unlocked it."

"You could have just knocked."

"Opening it was more fun. Don't worry, I come bearing good news."

James gulped some more beer. "Could use some, and you're certainly making enough money off me."

"Well, I'm earning it." Dannec sauntered over to the bar. "I'm beginning to understand the sigils."

"They weren't just some sort of self-destruct system?" Shay asked.

Dannec shook his head. "No, they are part of a magical energy channeling system. Relays to a sort of amplifier."

James frowned. "Amplifying what?"

"Could be a lot of things, but that's less important than understanding they *are* relays. I can potentially trace the magic now by experimenting with sigils of my own." Dannec pointed to some top-shelf vodka. "How about a little bonus for all my hard work, Tyler?"

Tyler eyed him for a second, the look on his face suggesting he was going to object, before grabbing the liquor and pouring a glass.

James nodded, the hint of a grin coming to his face. Finally, things were going their way. "You can trace it to the Council?"

"I can trace it to where it's being sent, and I doubt they'd be collecting energy just to make for an impressive little safehouse. There's a good chance they'll be at the target site." Dannec took a large drink of his vodka. "Ah, humans are good when it comes to spirits." He set the drink down. "But unfortunately, it's not all good news."

Tyler frowned. Maria and Shay looked annoyed.

The bounty hunter frowned. "Of course. What's the bad news?"

"If I'm not careful about this they might be able to trace it back to me, or I could blow myself up. It's going to take me a few days to get the artifacts I need to do this securely and safely and a few more after that to trace them, so about a week overall."

James grunted. "That's it? That's not bad news. That's just more time to prepare our ass-kicking surprise."

Dannec laughed. "Ah, that's the most interesting formulation of optimism I've ever come across." He picked his vodka up for another sip and offered an appreciative sigh.

Shay snickered and nodded to Maria. "If we're not going to go beat them down right away, I'm going to go show her a little something tomorrow. She needs better gear."

It couldn't be.

James stared at Shay. "You're gonna take her to a warehouse?"

She nodded. "It's not like she can use official AET gear, and if she's going to join us for the final party, I need to hook a sister up. We're gonna hit Warehouse Three tomorrow so she can do a little shopping."

"Your place. Your rules." He shrugged.

James picked up his beer and took a large gulp. The situation had changed in a matter of minutes. They might soon have the intelligence they needed. A week was plenty of time for additional training.

Not too late to surrender, you Council assholes.

The next morning, Trey and several other of the men crouched outside a massive maze-like construct of walls and raised towers. Small holes pierced the walls. It covered the area where the Camp Brownstone mud pit had been located previously.

Damn. Wonder if this means there'll be no more Mud King competitions.

"This is the shit you had people putting together when we were staking out those Council bastards?" Trey asked.

Royce chuckled. "James let me task the bulk of the remaining men with this little combat-engineering project. A little manual labor never hurt anyone. You guys are lucky you're not living in barracks where I can make you clean your toilets with toothbrushes."

The bounty hunters who'd been left behind all groaned.

"What the fuck *is* this thing?" Shorty asked. "Why ain't we just using the tactical room?"

"Because the tactical room is good for training, but it involves a lot of expensive gear. That means certain training options such as live-fire exercises wouldn't be a good idea." The DI pointed to the walls and towers. "Welcome to your new training environment, Fort Brownstone. James has informed me that you'll soon have to take on powerful magical foes. I don't have Alison here to throw spells at you, so I'm going to do my best to simulate magical attacks. I've been provided a few toys that'll help you see monsters to make it more realistic."

Shorty narrowed his eyes. "What the fuck you talking about, Staff Sergeant?"

"A little something James got from a supplier. You'll see some fucked-up monsters, and you'll go after them with live ammunition. You all need better psychological preparation for what you might see."

Trey laughed. "You're gonna drug our asses?"

"Something like that, but you won't be affected other than seeing the monsters. There'll be a spell that stops your bullets when they hit a monster. Some will be harder to 'kill.'" The DI headed toward the back door. "I'm going to go grab the potions. All of you get ready. The exercise will be simple. You'll navigate Fort Brownstone to the center. Take this shit seriously. For what the supplies for this exercise alone cost, he could probably afford to hire actual mercenaries instead of training your asses. James is doing this shit so you won't end up pissing your pants."

Royce marched toward the back door. "Be right back."

Trey rubbed his chin, thinking about the confrontation in Texas. He wondered if the only reason they hadn't lost it was that they couldn't see the monster clearly. Even then, not every man in the agency might have shown the fortitude his team had displayed. The training made sense.

He chuckled. "I don't think this shit's gonna go down as nicely as that bounty with Howard."

Shorty shook his head. "Still don't like that shit. Don't know why we had to go non-lethal against a bunch of fuckers with guns. We beat their asses, but it still wasn't a fair fight."

Lachlan snorted. "At least you got to beat someone down."

Trey shrugged. "Look, most bounties ain't dead or alive. Depending on who issued the bounty, if you end up killing them, you might only get half the money if you're lucky, or you get none of it. What good is being a motherfucking bounty hunter if you ain't getting paid?"

Shorty blinked. "Never thought much before why the big man doesn't just waste more people's asses. I just thought he didn't want us to come off like gangster thugs."

Royce appeared from the building holding a plastic bag filled with a dozen small bottles, each filled with a liquid and a small gemstone. "Line up and get your weapons ready. Oh, one last thing. I forgot to tell you that if you get too close to one of these *monsters* without disabling it, it'll make the shocks in the tactical room seem like a baby's slap in comparison, and you *will* piss yourself."

He hurled two bottles in rapid succession toward the nearest wall of Fort Brownstone and both shattered. The liquid vaporized in an instant, and their gems hovered in the air, turning slowly.

Trey narrowed his eyes. "That ain't look so scary."

Royce started chucking more bottles into Fort Brownstone. Before the rest even hit the ground, there was a bright flash from the first two gemstones.

Two ten-foot-tall giants with mottled flesh and three eyes replaced one of the gemstones. They let out loud roars.

Several of the men winced and stepped back.

A huge black widow, easily the size of Trey's F-350, replaced the other gem. More flashes occurred, and a menagerie of creatures appeared: skeletons, goblins, vampires, slithering masses of tentacles with human mouths but no eyes, weird-ass frogmen, four-armed blue-skinned demons with razor-sharp claws, and even several upright cockroaches with human eyes.

"That's some fucked-up shit," Trey muttered.

Royce laughed. "Yeah, it is. I suggest you start the battle, men." He pulled out his phone. "I forget to mention I'm giving you fifteen minutes to get to the center? If you don't get there by then, I'm going to throw in another bottle I have to simulate a Council self-destruct." He grinned. "Don't worry. It won't kill you, just really, really hurt you. James has authorized me to use healing potions for this exercise, so at least you won't die."

The men groaned in unison.

Trey adjusted his tie and pulled out his gun. "Time to kill me some monsters."

19

The good thing about having been a politician for decades was that it helped a man develop the important skill of smiling at a fool when said fool was running his damned mouth. Senator Johnston worked on finishing his salmon while his dining partner continued his latest rant.

Senator McNamara slammed a hand on the table. "What's the point of oversight if we're not actually providing oversight?"

Senator Johnston swallowed and took a sip of his water before responding. "How is the task force not being provided oversight?"

"The rest of the oversight committee hasn't gotten any reports out of the task force since Senator Silvers' arrest. You've been helping them run this operation like some sort of weird cowboy crap. And given the extensive resources being mobilized, I also fail to see why an Authorization for the Use of Military Force hasn't been voted on."

Senator Johnston chuckled. "This isn't a time to play

political games. The country's security's at stake. Hell, the *world's* security is at stake. It doesn't matter. Come on, Bobby. We've already had a vote that makes this all nice and legal."

The other senator narrowed his eyes. "I don't remember that. When, exactly?"

"They passed one fifteen years ago after that nonsense with the terrorist wizard. What his name? Yeah, Michael Galbraith." Johnston pulled out his phone and typed before clearing his throat. "Authorization for Use of United States Armed Forces and Relevant Support Personnel. In general, it says that the President is authorized to use all necessary and appropriate forces against those nations of either Earth or Oriceran, organizations, and/or persons he determines are planning, authorizing, committing, or aiding terrorist attacks related directly or indirectly to the wizard Michael Galbraith through use of magical or other enhanced means in order to prevent any future acts of international terrorism against the United States by such nations, organizations, or persons." He took a sip of water. "War Powers Resolution Requirements. (1) Consistent with section 8(a)(1) of the War Powers Resolution, the Congress declares that this section is intended to constitute specific statutory authorization within the meaning of section 5(b) of the War Powers Resolution with the 2022 addendum to redefine 'authorized forces to include both United States military forces, federally licensed bounty hunters, and federally licensed private military contractors."

Senator McNamara stared at him dumbfounded. "Michael Galbraith's dead. The Council doesn't have anything to do with him."

"Now, we don't know that." Senator Johnston shrugged with a smile.

"You're abusing a statute that was targeted toward a particular individual's organization as an excuse to run a black op using federal resources and a dangerously unpredictable bounty hunter. This is beyond absurd. It goes to the point of parody."

Senator Johnston laughed. "When you say it like that it sounds so sordid. This isn't some killing innocent peasants in a village thing, Bobby. This is stopping a bunch of dangerous people who weren't above assassinating the Chairman of the Joint Chiefs of Staff. Get some damned perspective."

Senator McNamara shook his head, his face reddening. "Given everything I've heard about James Brownstone, I'm sure he's breaking laws and causing countless unjustified deaths. Quite frankly, if you're not going to provide oversight, then you should know that all of the people involved in this will pay for their flouting of the law and the death and destruction they're responsible for."

"I assure you that no unnecessary death or destruction is going on."

The other man leaned forward and narrowed his eyes. "Then why can't you give us reports? Even a single one? What are you hiding? What is Brownstone hiding? There should be an immediate halt to this operation until we get more reports."

Senator Johnston offered him a placating smile. "You'll forgive me if after having a member of the task force assassinated and discovering another is working for the terrorists, I'm reticent to spread our information all over. Congress leaks like a sieve."

The other senator stood and shook his head. "Thanks for the lunch, Bill. I'm not going to keep yelling at you about it, but I also want you to know that I'm not letting this go. I will stop this operation if you refuse oversight."

"Do what you need to do. We all serve the country in our own way."

Senator Johnston watched as his colleague stormed out of the restaurant. Once the other man had left the building, the senator picked up his phone and texted a quick message.

Thirty seconds later, his phone rang and he answered it. "Meet me at Calabrese in an hour. I have a favor to ask."

Shay smirked as Maria walked through Warehouse Three behind her, shaking her head. "Sorry about the blindfold, but I guess I only trust you ninety percent, not a hundred percent. Old habits die hard."

Maria eyed the shelves and racks of weapons and equipment filling the room and whistled. "When you told me the other night about having a warehouse filled with weapons, I thought you had a storage unit stocked with some boxes, not a literal *warehouse*."

"This is just one of them. I've got different types: one with workout gear, another with my magic stuff, and my library. Warehouse Two's kind of my office. That's where Peyton hangs out."

The cop eyed her. "Wait, your library? You've got an entire warehouse filled with books?"

Shay nodded. "Yes. Rare books. It's the only warehouse I won't let James see."

"So you'll let him know where your magical artifact warehouse is, but you won't let him see your library?"

"Yeah. Those are irreplaceable books. He'll probably walk in there and get sticky barbeque sauce on them." Shay shrugged.

Maria laughed as she walked over to shelves containing boxes with different types of grenades. "I think you have almost as many weapons as the entire LAPD in here. I get that you used to kill people for a living and you're a tomb raider now, but isn't this overkill?"

Shay shook her head. "It's good to be prepared. When I go on a tomb raid, it might be as simple as digging something up from the back of an old warehouse, or it might involve me having to fight magical monsters underwater." She moved over to a gun rack and ran her hand over a few rifles. "Also, in some cases, they might be night missions, or they could be something where I'm dragging equipment around for days in the middle of the jungle, and I need to take weight into account. Not everything's a quick in-and-out."

The cop grimaced. "Ugh. Seriously?"

Shay nodded and motioned around. "I don't keep my magical gear in here, but you're welcome to borrow any of this stuff. I don't have the kind of heavy armor you use in AET, but I've got armor. I do have a few defensive artifacts I'll bring along, so that'll help us, in addition to the anti-magic deflector."

Maria moved over toward the rifles. "Lots of rifles, but no railguns?"

The tomb raider shook her head. "I used to have some, but I got rid of them. I don't like them. Too unwieldy and unreliable. If I need something big and powerful, I prefer explosives."

Maria laughed. "Thanks for agreeing to help me out. I found out this morning they've accepted my leave of absence."

"You really sure you have to go that far?"

The cop nodded. "There's just too much paperwork to do and permissions I have to get otherwise, and these Council bastards are dangerous and kidnapped me, so yeah. I guess I'm channeling my inner Brownstone and ready for a little revenge."

Shay snickered. "Yeah, I don't know half the time if being with him has made me more dangerous or less dangerous."

"Dangerous, huh? After all that stuff you told me about history, you telling me you've never seriously thought about just settling down and doing less dangerous work?" Maria grabbed a nice Steyr off a rack and inspected it with a longing gaze. "If you can afford multiple warehouses filled with gear, I imagine it's not exactly like you need to work."

"I ask myself that question a lot." Shay shrugged and moved over to a shelf containing vests and armor. "Some people might say I'm addicted to danger in the end. I could be. Maybe that's why I'm dating someone like James."

Maria laughed. "Yeah, Tyler may be a bit of a scumbag, but he's really not that dangerous."

Shay took a deep breath. "Just so you know, very few people have ever been to this place, blindfolded or otherwise."

"Yeah. I get that. I know we're kind of friends, but I'm still surprised that you'd show me all this stuff. For all you know, I could get mad and decide to bust you for all these illegal weapons."

The tomb raider chuckled and shook her head. "If I'm going to trust you to have my back, then I need to make sure you don't have a damned pee shooter when we're firing at a charging demon."

Maria eyed her. "So you're saying it's just self-preservation?"

"I'm saying that's what I tell myself so I can sleep at night."

"I've got your back whether you like it or not." Maria smirked. "But trusting a cop makes you nervous and restless?"

"Don't feel too bad. It used to be that trusting *anyone* made me nervous and restless." Shay reached under her jacket and pulled out one of her adamantine knives. "This was custom-made by a gnome. Pretty damned sharp, although not as powerful as the magic sword I'm going to bring to the party." She held it out hilt-first. "But sometimes you just have to stab a motherfucker. But if you lose that, you might as well let them eat you, because I'll have to kill you."

Maria blinked, then grinned. The women shared a laugh.

Senator Johnston smiled at the young man in a hoodie who sat across from him in his booth. He waited to speak until the man had pulled out a small coin and set in on the table.

"We good?" he asked.

The man nodded. "Yeah. No one can hear us." He glanced to his side. "Good choice on the seating; no good visuals on our mouths. You don't have any idea how refreshing it is to work with a proper professional again. Half these fools think we're in a spy novel but want to shout from the rooftops that they're doing something secret."

Senator Johnston chuckled. "Happy this old fart can impress you, son. Are you still going by Galahad these days, or do you have a new handle or nickname or whatever you call it?"

"Galahad's fine." The hacker glanced over his shoulder. "So, let's get down to business. Yeah, I already had a file on McNamara. I was keeping it in my back pocket in case I needed it."

"With all the scum in Congress, you must have a mighty big back pocket."

The hacker smirked. "You could say that."

The senator shot him another smile, picked up his cup of coffee, and took a sip. "I thought he was dirty. Men that strident are usually trying to hide how damned filthy they are."

Galahad snorted. "He isn't even a *good* dirtbag. The asshole barely covers his tracks. Bribes all over the place. Hell, he's taking bribes from opposing sides at times."

"That's unfortunate." Senator Johnston clucked his

tongue. "You know what defines a *good* corrupt congressman?"

"What?"

"He stays bought when someone bribes him."

Galahad tapped his phone and spun it around to show the senator.

The older man frowned. "That's a highly classified matter, son. Why are you showing me this now?"

"Just a sample of some of the info McNamara's been selling on the dark web."

Senator Johnston sighed. "That's just disappointing. Being greedy is bad enough, but selling out your country? Some things a patriot can't forgive. Now I'm going to be forced to handle him in an unpleasant manner."

Galahad shrugged. "You would have anyway. I've traced at least one bribe to an account associated with the Council."

"Why am I not surprised?" The senator shook his head.

The hacker took his phone back and put in his pocket. "How do you plan to handle him?"

"I don't want this leaking back to me." Senator Johnston rubbed the back of his neck. "Too much sensitive crap going on right now, and I don't have time for hearings and accusations. With the Senator Silvers incident, both her arrest and her death in jail, there's a lot of people who want to pull the rug out from under this whole operation just for their own political gain. I've got a damned country to save, and unlike that asshole, I'm not willing to sell it out for a few extra dollars. This bastard needs to be taken care of, so let's do a shell game here."

Galahad furrowed his brow. “Not following you, Senator.”

“I have some people working for me right now. They’ve got hackers working for them, too. Very skilled. I’d like it if your information about our mutual friend made it to them. They can then decide how they want to handle it. They are very interested in not being told what to do by the government, so they might not even come to me with the information.”

“Okay. Sure.” The hacker nodded. “I can set up a series of hints—breadcrumbs—that if they’re good enough, they’ll be able to follow until they find the information. I’ll also set some stuff up so I can get a good fingerprint of them. They might be helping you now, but they might sell you out later.”

Senator Johnston chuckled. “Fine, son. That sounds like a good plan. Just don’t do anything to piss them off. Their bosses… Well, let’s just say we wouldn’t like how they’d handle the situation if they thought the government was coming after them..”

Galahad blinked, obvious surprise on his face. “Your call.”

The senator rubbed his hands together. “Always fun taking down a traitor.”

20

Peyton frowned and tilted his head. "What the hell is this?"

Heather blinked. "Something wrong with the frame rate on my camera?"

He shook his head and double-checked her video feed just in case. "No, no, no. It's just that I was looking up some additional Council financial stuff, and I found a reference to an offshore account I hadn't seen before. You know we've been so up their butts that I feel like I'm the IRS auditing them."

"So what's the deal?"

"An account number with a crypto bank," Peyton replied. "They've got it concealed to make it look like it's just some Andercarr corporate delivery contract stuff, but I recognized the signature. Someone's been moving a lot of Bitcoin and Trollcoin around, it looks like."

"Do you have an address?"

Peyton nodded. He clicked a few times to send her the information. "Let's chase this thing down."

Several hours later, Peyton wiped the sweat from his brow. "Any luck?"

Heather sighed and shook her head. "Same thing. I could follow it from the crypto bank through the secondary payment processor, then back to the phone and then to the IP address, but it ends up in some ridiculously secure DoD server. I can't find a way in that won't get us tagged. Shit. Am I just missing something obvious?"

Peyton sighed. "Nope. I've hacked DoD servers, but this one's just too locked down. If we press, we're going to tip them off."

"What the heck do we do, then?"

Peyton pulled out his phone. "We can't access it remotely, so somebody's going to need to get in there physically. At least we know where it is, even if we can't get to it."

Heather frowned. "What good does that do?"

"I know people who are good at breaking into places." He winked and dialed Shay.

"What's up?" she answered on the first ring.

Peyton cleared his throat. "We found some information on a senator who might be connected to the Council. He isn't involved with the task force, but he might be trouble. The problem is that the final proof is on a server we can't access remotely without getting tagged, but we know the data is there. Like physically, even down to the room. Maybe you could go do your thing and get it, then we check it out, and you know, conveniently leak it to the media or something to take care of him." He sighed. "And before you think about just saying, 'Why don't I kill him?' remember this guy's a United States senator."

Shay laughed. "I wasn't planning on killing him. Well, not yet. Hell, I didn't even kill the guy who helped fuck with Alison's adoption. Okay, you and Heather leave it alone. Send me the location information, and I'll get it handled."

"*Without* killing a senator?" Peyton verified.

"Yes. I've still got a few people I can ask for favors. Non-murder favors, too."

The Professor chugged his latest pint in one mighty gulp. The crowd at the Leanan Sídhe was surprisingly subdued. It was like the entire bar could sense his mood despite the smile on his face.

I'm not nearly drunk enough to be saving the world yet again. I thought I'd be able to retire by now. She had the right idea about this.

He slapped his cheeks. Brooding didn't suit him. It was like he was turning into James.

The Professor chuckled at the thought and looked down at his ready second mug of beer. When he looked up, Correk was standing in front of him.

"A good evening to you, my old friend," the Professor offered.

The elf smiled and took a seat. "You said it was urgent, so I'm here."

"Aye. Council-related business. The hacking team working for James needs some information on a Department of Defense server. They can't access it remotely, so they need someone to go and connect this transmitter to the computer." He reached into his pocket and set a tiny black square in front of him. "More importantly, they need it to happen without anyone knowing right away. Maybe with more time, Miz Carson might be able to do it, but they're very close to honing in on the Council base. I'd rather them not be distracted from that. I thought someone with a magical touch might have a better chance."

Correk sighed and shrugged. "I *could* do it, but if they start looking around and suspect magic, they'll get the PDA involved. I've crossed paths with them enough that if they examine the relevant area, they'll recognize my magical signature. That'll draw a lot of attention to me, and make my job a lot harder in the future. You know how uneasy my relationships with most governments on Earth are at times, let alone the American one."

The Professor chuckled and took a sip. "Aye, of course. Is there someone else you can use?"

A broad smile covered the elf's face.

Why do I have a bad feeling about this?

"How about someone who is smart, small, but large when he needs to be, and sneaky?" Correk grinned. "Now, if I can get him to do this and not moon the cameras, we'll be golden."

The Professor groaned and scrubbed his face with his hand. "Just keep him away from the Cheetos."

"Give a man a slice of pizza, and he'll eat for a day," Peyton declared solemnly. "Teach a man to cook pizza, and he'll eat for life."

Heather snorted. "Unless he doesn't have the money for the ingredients. Bad analogy."

"You're just jealous that I'm the Pizza King."

"I don't even like pizza that much."

Peyton gasped. "Blasphemy. *Lèse-majesté.*"

Heather rolled her eyes and opened her mouth, then frowned and looked down at her computer. Peyton looked at his second screen. An alert had popped up.

"It's data being transmitted through the proxy chain," he commented. "Wait, from the transmitter? That was quick."

Heather laughed. "Yeah, I thought that would take a few days to pull off."

Peyton clicked on the data dump file and started skimming through it. Heather did the same on her end.

A few minutes passed before Peyton broke the silence. "Woah."

Heather blinked several times. "Damn. This guy is dirty even by the standards of a congressman. Maybe Shay *should* kill him."

Peyton shook his head. "I've got a better idea. Let's make some mid-level reporter's day."

Heather laughed. "What you mean?"

"I'm just saying, it's time for us to mail a little anonymous dirt to a reporter and then the FBI. The reporter will start pressuring the FBI right away, and they'll move. We've got all the evidence in a nice little package. Senator McNamara's arrested in a day or two tops, and whatever shit he's doing for the Council stops."

The other hacker eyed Peyton through the camera. "You've got a ruthless streak, don't you?"

He grinned. "Shay's rubbing off on me."

21

Crazak tilted his head as he examined the sprawling gated complex in Amsterdam through a scrying window. "Even with the raids on some of the energy nodes, we still have sufficient reserves to move forward with the backup plan. I suggest we do so."

Yilin frowned and put her hand down on the table. A thin sheet of ice spread several inches from her fingers. "The receivers haven't been fully calibrated. And what of all the energy we've sent to this facility? The energy flow is stronger in this part of America than it'll be in Amsterdam. We all agreed this place in Wyoming would be the superior location for our headquarters because of that. How can we change now? It'd be a tremendous waste."

The elf snorted. "They've been hitting our safe houses and nodes one by one. It's only a matter of time before they find this place and assault it. The government's dogs are more persistent than we anticipated, but they've struck nowhere but the United States, so their reach is obviously limited. Relocating to Amsterdam is a less elegant solution than we prefer, I agree, but it's not worth further losses. We must think long-term."

Ferrao folded his hands in front of him on the other side of the table. "I agree." He frowned and looked around. "Where is He Who Hunts?"

Crazak shook his head. "I've not seen him for days. His minions are still proceeding with their orders, and he's reinforced many of the transmission sigils in Asia. I've contacted him, and he's informed me that he's 'harvesting in preparation for the move.'"

Yilin frowned. "You're sure he isn't abandoning us?"

"If he is, he'll learn what true fear is, but if he were to do such a thing, there would be no reason for him to continue to reinforce the sigils." Crazak smiled. "I suggest we move within the week. We should make preparations to retune the receivers in Amsterdam. Do either of you have any objections?"

The gnome and the frostling shook their heads.

Crazak nodded. "Good. He Who Hunts didn't see fit to be present, so he forfeits his vote. We shall retreat to Amsterdam to rebuild our strength, and then we shall return to punish the forces in the United States that dared oppose us. They will learn that they were merely fortunate before."

He lifted his hand and squeezed it into a fist.

James was about to cut into a steak when his phone buzzed with a text from Dannec. He picked it up.

I have their location.

Coordinates appeared.

Something's fluctuating though. Whatever you're going to do, you should do it fast.

The bounty hunter grunted and took a bite of his steak. He texted back.

Thanks. We'll handle it ASAP.

James put the coordinates into a map app. They took him to mountains east of Devil's Tower in Wyoming. When he checked the satellite images, there was nothing but normal mountains there.

Government contacts scrubbing the data, or magical cloaking? Fuck it. Need to move on this. Maybe after I score our transportation, I can get Dannec to help with recon.

He dialed Senator Johnston.

"Hello, son," the senator answered. "Tell me you've got good news."

"It's time to end this shit," James rumbled. "I just need you to help me get my team from LA to Wyoming."

The senator chuckled. "That's the easy part. The hard part will be facing them."

"Don't worry. I'll handle that."

Shay yawned and glanced around the interior of the massive Air Force plane. The rumble made it hard to hear much of the chatter from the others in the plane. It was the largest team she'd ever worked with. Besides James and Maria, the dozens of men who formed the rank and file of the Brownstone Agency filled the seats. It was a damned army.

James' words from weeks ago floated to the top of her mind.

This isn't going to be a tomb raid anyway. This is fucking war.

Maria took a deep breath in the seat next to Shay.

"Don't like flying?" Shay asked.

"No, it's not that. Just…" She shrugged. "I lost a man to these bastards the last time. It's fucking me up. I don't know if you'd call it PTSD or just anger."

"Nothing wrong with wanting a little revenge for your man." Shay looked forward. James sat in the front row, a frown on his face and earbuds in. Even he looked a little pale.

My poor ass-kicking baby.

She wasn't surprised. The man hated flying, even in service of a nice righteous beatdown.

Shay shook her head. "This isn't like that. This is like the final time we faced those museum bastards. We had James on our side then, and now we don't just have James, we have a whole army of bounty hunters too. Way more guys than you had when you lost your man."

Maria nodded. "It's why I took the leave of absence. I had to be here. I want to be able to go back to his widow and look her straight in the eye and tell her, 'The people who were ultimately responsible for this have faced justice.' Then she can have closure, and he can rest in peace." She scrubbed a hand over her face. "Hell, I can *sleep* in peace."

Shay patted her shoulder. "If there's one thing James and I are good at, it's kicking ass. We'll get your revenge."

"I hope so, and... What the hell is he doing?"

Shay looked to the front. James had stood and pulled out his earbuds. He walked to the front of the cabin and stood in the center aisle.

"Listen up," he shouted. His booming voice defeated the rumble of the plane.

Everyone's heads snapped forward. The men sleeping shot awake.

James grunted and surveyed the room. "We've got about twenty minutes until we land in Ellsworth. A little reminder in case any of you people weren't paying attention before. From there, they're taking us by VTOL insertion craft toward the site but outside the Council shield. The government's going to man the perimeter, and PDA witches and wizards are gonna do some shit so there won't be any portals. Unless we take out the Council, the shields they put around the base will stop any direct missile attacks or any shit like that. So this is going to be brutal, direct, in-their-face shit." He slammed his fist into his palm. "This isn't dead or alive. This is just dead. This is war, and we're gonna annihilate these assholes."

The bounty hunters raised their fists in the air and cheered.

Shay arched a brow.

Damn, James is really pumping these guys up.

"You've been training with Staff Sergeant Royce," James continued. "You've gotten used to shooting at weird shit. Make no mistake, this isn't gonna be like any bounty you've ever faced. Don't take anyone or anything you see there lightly, or you might get killed."

"Or get shot in your balls," Shorty shouted.

Everyone burst into laughter.

James chuckled. "Or get shot in your balls." He tapped on his phone, and a moment later the large screen at the front of the passenger cabin came to life and displayed an image of a sprawling and rugged complex of buildings in the mountains.

Everyone leaned forward.

"An elf friend was nice enough to get this image for us." He gestured toward it and tapped different large letters. "You all know your teams. The government and my elf friend have confirmed there are more than a few people at the site, but we don't know anything about the inside. At least one Council member has been confirmed to be there, an elf named Crazak. If he's there, the others probably are too." He frowned. "Just like the government can't bomb the fuck out of the place, because of the shield we're not going to be able to do any funny drone tricks. Make sure that when you get off this plane, you have all your gear and you have double-checked your damned potions. Don't waste your anti-magic bullets on regular targets.

"Remember Lieutenant Hall's briefing about the anti-magic deflectors. If they get too dark, you need to pull back. The only people dying today will be the Council and their lackeys." He turned off the display. "We don't know how many monsters or soldiers the Council have left.

We've picked off a lot of places and grabbed some artifacts, but this will be their last stand, and they will fight like cornered animals. So watch each other's fucking backs, and make sure that every last Council motherfucker goes to meet their maker. Understood?"

The men all cheered.

Shay smiled. With an army like this, how could they lose?

22

Whispy Doom was thrilled about the upcoming battle, and he refused to not make that very clear to James.

Kill strong enemies. Adapt. Grow stronger. Reach advanced transformation. Full capabilities yet to be unlocked.

James grunted. *Yeah. Lots of killing coming soon. I don't give a shit about my full capabilities there, Coach.*

Coach is incorrect designation.

He glanced over his shoulder. All his men plus Maria and Shay walked behind him. Air Force trucks had brought them to the edge of the Council's defenses. He wasn't sure how they knew but assumed the PDA was involved.

He didn't care that much about the Council's defenses, other than that they prevented Heather and Peyton from backing them up with drones. From what the military had told him, there were no conventional transmissions going in or out of the invisible dome surrounding the Council facility. There would be no fancy communications tech this time.

Comes to boots on the ground in the end. Always does when you really need to get shit done.

The main buildings were already in sight. The battle that had started weeks ago was now just minutes from continuing.

Fucking Council. Should have known better than to pick a fight with the United States of America and me.

Trey jogged up to James' side. Instead of his signature suit, he, like all the men, was clad head to toe in a black tactical outfit complete with kneepads, combat boots, and a helmet.

They weren't going after bounties. They were fighting a war, and they needed to dress accordingly.

They do look pretty badass.

James chuckled. He wasn't wearing anything special other than one of his shabby gray coats. This time he just wanted the additional pocket space for more death-dealing goodies. His tactical harness and belt couldn't hold enough grenades. He patted the rocket launcher slung over his shoulder, his "door key," as he thought of it.

"Any last-minute word from the military?" Trey asked.

James nodded. "They told me the Council pulled all its forces inside, so they know we're coming. I never figured we could surprise them anyway. I like it better this way. I want them to sweat."

Trey frowned. "And you're sure they're not running? Hate to get all dressed up for the prom only to find out it was canceled."

"No, the PDA assured me they've got that covered." James shrugged. "Some specialist helped them, but they wouldn't tell me. I didn't care that much, so I didn't press them on it."

A knowing look crossed Shay's face, but she didn't say anything.

Do I even want to know? Whatever. We're here, and we'll kick ass. Answers can come later if we need them.

James slowed as the mountain path gave way to concrete. The Council hadn't even bothered with a fence. He wasn't sure if that was confidence or arrogance.

He pointed to a large central building. "From what I was told, the Council's men are in there. We'll stick to the earlier plan. I'm gonna knock on their door to get their attention with Shay's and Lieutenant Hall's help. The other two teams should hit the sides and sweep toward the center. Pincer-attack shit. I'm sure Royce would be proud."

The Brownstone Army advanced along the concrete, no one saying a thing. The crystals of their anti-magic deflectors bounced lightly against their chest armor. At Royce's suggestion, James had decided against bulletproof vests to focus on armor with more resistance to stabbing and slashing. They expected monsters and magic, not gunslingers.

Although every man carried a holstered pistol, they moved toward the building with loaded and ready assault rifles. A few men, like James, were also lugging RPGs or rocket launchers. Shay was the only person with a sword belt, but all the men at least had a single knife, if not two.

James halted about twenty yards from the front of the building. Two massive metal doors stood there, decorated with two halves of an elaborate crest made up of concentric circles and upside-down triangles.

This magical shit? Guess we'll see if it can take a rocket.

"Teams spread out," James bellowed.

Trey and half the bounty hunters rushed toward one side of the building. Shorty led the other half toward the opposite side.

Insufficient power for advanced transformation, Whispy Doom rattled inside James' mind.

I don't need that shit yet.

Killing enemies with normal weapons insufficient for growth.

Sometimes kicking ass the old-fashioned way is good enough, and I don't like what it does to my head to get to sufficient power.

Sufficient power is necessary for advanced transformation.

Fuck off, Coach.

James pulled the rocket launcher off his shoulder and lined it up with the front door. "Here's a present, motherfuckers."

The rocket hissed away from the launcher and smashed into the front door, blowing shrapnel into the air. Smoke and flames covered the doors, and after a few seconds, they fell to the ground with a hollow booming thud.

Blasts from both sides of the building followed a few seconds later, along with the shouts of the men.

Let's do this shit.

James pulled out his rifle and charged with a bellow.

Shay and Maria rushed after him, their rifles ready.

The trio hit the doorway and pushed through the smoke to find dozens of four-armed Zains waiting, snapping their teeth and twitching their claws with murder in their eyes

Insufficient power for advanced transformation.

Shut the fuck up. I don't need that shit for these assholes.

James didn't fire the rifle. Instead, he grabbed a frag

grenade and chucked it into the mass of waiting killers. Shay grinned and copied his strategy, but Maria opened fire.

The monsters charged, the grenades exploding in their midst. One fell to a tight burst of bullets to the head. James kept throwing grenades while Maria kept flinging bullets into the monsters, a grim smile on her face.

Payback, huh?

The growls of men, explosions, and gunfire echoed down the hall from either side. The Brownstone Army was fully engaged with the enemy.

Several Zains closed on James. He whipped out his Ka-Bar and dodged to the left of the charging mob, his heart rate speeding up.

Maria snorted. "Seriously, Brownstone?" She kept spewing bullets to the right, while Shay took more careful shots at creatures in the center of the horde.

Despite the cop's snort, she had to stab a closing Zain when her rifle ran dry with a monster a yard away.

She pulled out the knife and eyed it. "Nice."

A monster slashed at James, its claws stinging but leaving only a small scratch. The bounty hunter's coat and shirt took more damage than he did.

James slammed his knife into a Zain's head and yanked it out. The creature fell to the ground, its blood spurting into the air. He kicked another creature back a few yards before spinning to stab a new one in the neck. He followed up by planting his knife through its eye.

Whispy Doom's thoughts took on a more harried quality. *Kill lesser enemies and advance. Find stronger enemies. Kill and adapt. Insufficient power for advanced transformation. Full transformation potential has been readied.*

Shut the fuck up and let me do my thing.

The Zain swarm shifted direction, with most now rushing toward James. Maria kept firing and reloading, dropping monster after monster. Shay managed to nail the back line with more grenades, but she didn't have that many left.

They'd winnowed the dozens of monsters down to a single dozen.

James let out a roar and pulled out a second knife, then charged the advancing Zains and slashed and stabbed. The desperate beasts clawed and bit with wild abandon, but the lake of blood forming on the floor wasn't from James Brownstone, who had only scratches.

A final Zain tried to tackle the bounty hunter, and he slammed his elbow down on its neck with a loud thud and crunch. It fell to the ground but kept raking his legs with its claws, so he sheathed his knives and pulled out his .45 instead of his rifle. He aimed it at the creature's head and emptied the gun into it until nothing remained.

James booted the rest of the Zain, and it tumbled through the air before landing with a soft, squishy thud on a pile of four-armed bodies.

The bounty hunter stared at the dead creatures and gritted his teeth, dark feelings from Shay's kidnapping returning.

"Is that all you've got?" James roared. "Bad-ass Council, huh? You sent me a bunch of piece-of-shit monsters that couldn't take down an LA street gang made up of thirteen-year-olds?" He pounded his chest. "You came into *my* city.

Killed people there. Kidnapped my friends and girlfriend. Why don't you pussies actually come out and fight me?"

Yes, the amulet hissed. *Increase power for advanced transformation.*

Shay pointed toward a hall leading deep into the building. "We're going to have to dig them out. I don't think just taunting them is gonna work."

Maria inspected her weapon. "We should wait for the other teams. Don't want to get flanked and surrounded."

James let out a low growl. He didn't want to kill peons. He wanted the bosses' heads.

Fight stronger enemies for maximum adaptation.

Fuck that. I don't give a shit about what you want. I just want to make the Council pay for thinking they can do whatever the fuck they want in LA and the country.

Then increase power for advanced transformation. Insufficient power.

James grunted and resisted the urge to run straight down the hall. Gunfire and shouts still came from both sides.

"Getting there in terms of power," he mumbled.

Shay looked at him. "What?"

"Don't worry about it. Just having an argument with myself."

Trey wiped some Zain blood off his face. "Fuck. What if these bastards have demon gonorrhea or some shit? Gonna have to get shots for the rest of my life."

Glad I didn't wear a suit to this shit.

"Just don't swallow," Manuel yelled. He put a few rounds into one of the remaining monsters, which stumbled to the ground and rolled a few feet from its momentum. The bounty hunter's concentrated fire blew several of its limbs off.

Tough, but not as tough as our boss.

The bounty hunters looked at the tangle of limbs and bodies. T.J. had taken a nasty scratch to his side but was already back up and operational with the help of a painkiller.

"These ain't that freaky," Isaiah commented. He kicked a dead Zain. "Not compared to the shit Staff Sergeant was making us see."

Trey grinned. "That's the point. If we had done this shit a few weeks ago, we would have all been freaked out and these bastards would have torn our throats out. Maybe you won't bitch so much next time James and Staff Sergeant give us special training."

He narrowed his eyes at shadows moving along a far wall and whipped up his rifle.

Six men with wands turned the corner.

The bounty hunters opened fire. A shield around the wizards flashed when they were hit, and the bullets bounced to the ground, crushed.

A few of the wizards grinned.

You ain't won yet, motherfuckers.

"Fall back," Trey shouted. He pulled out a grenade and threw it. "Flashbang in."

He turned away, waited for the explosion, and then snapped his attention back to the enemies. The wizards weren't swaying or clutching their eyes.

They looked straight ahead and raised their wands. Green and red bolts blasted toward the bounty hunters, missing several, but one nailing Manuel. He screamed and fell to the ground.

Shit.

A red bolt slammed into an invisible shield around Trey, its energy spreading and thinning over the shell until it disappeared.

He glanced down at the locket hanging underneath the still clear anti-magic deflector.

Thanks, Zoe.

"Switch mags!" he ordered. "And light those motherfuckers up!"

The men all ejected their conventional rounds and slapped in anti-magic rounds. Another volley from the wizards knocked two more bounty hunters to the ground. The scent of burnt nylon and cotton poplin filled the hallway.

Damn you, wizard motherfuckers. You ain't all that.

Trey brought up his reloaded rifle and switched to full auto. "Eat this, bitches!" He held the trigger down and swept the weapon back and forth.

The smug look on the wizards' faces disappeared as the bounty hunters' bullets pierced their shields and ripped into their bodies. The six wizards jerked, struggling to stay upright. Several fell against the wall clutching their wounds, blood pouring from them.

"Ain't so tough now, are you, bitches?" Trey's clip ran dry, and he nodded to the other bounty hunters. "Finish those bitches off."

Daryl, Kevin, and Charles advanced in front of him,

squeezing off single shots that cut through their enemies. Without their shields, the wizards would have been killed by the first volley, but their magic didn't save them from the enchanted bullets now shredding them.

Their perforated bodies fell to the ground.

Trey threw his rifle over his shoulder and rushed to Manuel. The large hole in his shirt and singed skin didn't look promising.

Damn it.

The man sat up with a groan and shook his head. "It felt more like getting hit with a stun rifle." He glanced down at his anti-magic deflector, which was now murky brown in color. "Guess this shit saved my life."

Trey grinned. "At least they didn't shoot you in the dick."

The other wounded men sat up, looking a little pale but not injured. Their anti-magic deflectors were also darkened.

"Come on," Trey shouted. "We need to go hook up with the big man's team."

23

James grunted as Trey's team rushed into the main room. Shorty's showed up less than thirty seconds later. Several men had been shot or wounded, judging by the burns and holes in their clothes along with darkened deflectors, and a few were bloody, but no one looked seriously injured.

The guys are being smart about their deflectors and healing potions.

"Any trouble?" he asked.

"Just those Zains and some wizard bitches," Trey explained. "But we're alive and they ain't, so you know how *that* shit went down."

Shorty snorted. "We didn't even get no monsters on our side. Just a bunch of wizards and fuckers with this explodin' rock shit. What's up with that?"

Shay shook her head and wiped the blood off her face. "Don't get too cocky. This was just a test. They're using disposable forces to judge our strength and make us run through our supplies. It's only gonna get harder from here."

Shorty shrugged. "Fine by me. Bring me a dragon so I can kill it and become Sir Shorty the Dragon slayer."

The men laughed.

Shay and Maria smirked.

"Let's get going," James shouted. "There are still far too many fuckers who aren't us and are still breathing around here."

The Brownstone Army jogged down the hall, already a bloody mess, even if that blood was mostly from their enemies. They hit a three-way intersection with no additional foes in sight.

Fucking Council. Just stop being pussies, already.

James frowned and pointed to his left and then his right. "Brownstone Agency, go left. Shay and Lieutenant Hall, you go right. I'll go forward. If you get into trouble, send someone for me, and I'll back you up."

Shay eyed him. "You're going by yourself? You think that's a good idea?"

He grunted. "I can handle myself."

Find enemy, the amulet whispered. *Increase power for advanced transformation.*

Maria and Shay exchanged looks, and both rolled their eyes.

I don't have time to debate if you think this is a big dick thing. Just fucking listen to me.

The women didn't say anything, just jogged to the side corridor.

"Thank you," he mumbled under his breath.

Trey gave a little grin and led his men to the opposite side.

James pulled down his rifle and charged forward.

Good. This way, if I need to lose it, there's no chance I'll hurt any of my people.

He grunted.

I'm coming for you, Council.

Shay hurried down the seemingly endless and featureless hall.

What was that?

She jerked to a stop and flattened herself against the wall. Maria didn't question her and mirrored her movements.

The tomb raider tilted her head and listened. She could hear an oscillating buzzing sound from around the corner, and she doubted they'd stumbled onto an electrical transformer in the middle of a series of halls.

She pulled out a couple of grenades and nodded at Maria. The cop brought up her rifle and grinned.

Shay took a deep breath, pulled the pins, and then spun around the corner to toss the grenades.

"What the fuck?"

Her grenades disintegrated without exploding when they slammed into a shimmering yellow field extending across the hallway, emanating from tall glowing rods on either side. A gnome encased in what appeared to be a suit of jade armor stood opposite the field, smirking. Instead of hands, wide barrels tipped the arms of the suit. A solid faceplate lay right above his eyes.

Fuck. I doubt he's just wearing that as a fashion statement.

Maria fired a few rounds. The bullets also disintegrated.

"I am Ferrao of the Council," he declared. "I'll give you a bit of credit for tracking us here and surviving our little presents."

"I'm Shay Carson and this is Maria Hall." She nodded toward the cop. "You're gonna be dead real soon, though, so I guess this shit is just wasting time, right?"

"Perhaps." The gnome shook his head. "You could be useful. I sense you're not like the other tools the government has sent against us. The Council offers wealth and power if you serve us competently."

Shay groaned. "It doesn't matter what species it is, men always want to give a big speech about how badass they are." She reached into a pouch and pulled out a small tied-off bag. "You gonna fight, or are you gonna try and bore us to death, Ferrao?"

The gnome shrugged. "You'll never make it past the culling field, so it doesn't matter. I'll just wait until all your friends are dead and hunt you with the others. This is the problem with you humans. You have no patience." He snorted. "I'm amazed your species has advanced as far as it has."

Maria looked at Shay, an eyebrow raised in question. The tomb raider shot her back a huge grin.

Time to bag me a Council member.

Shay nodded. "You're right about one thing, Ferrao. I'm not a very patient human at times." She tossed the bag at the field.

He rolled his eyes. "Please. You're embar—"

The field vaporized the bag, and a cloud of shimmering

dust blasted out. On contact with the field, it spread in a purple wave. A second later, the two glowing rods crumbled to dust and the yellow field disappeared.

The gnome took several steps backward, his eyes wide. The faceplate fell over his eyes.

Can he even see in that thing?

"Impossible," the gnome exclaimed.

Shay aimed her rifle. "That's the problem with you Council assholes. You got too used to dealing with soldiers and bounty hunters. Guys who aren't always the most flexible."

"And what are you, then?"

She grinned. "I'm a tomb raider, asshole."

Maria and Shay opened fire, and their bullets sparked and bounced off the gnome's armor. Bright white orbs grew with a low rumble in his barrels. The women ducked around opposite corners as he blasted two shots off.

The shots slammed into the walls behind Shay, blowing a huge chunk out of the wall. The shockwave knocked her to her knees, but she just shook her head and stood.

Okay, he can see well enough to shoot.

"I've been wanting to test this," the gnome yelled. "It was worthless, you see, until I got my hands on an artifact from that museum. I can't wait to improve it."

Maria pulled out a sonic grenade and tossed it around the corner. The telltale whine sounded a moment later, but the gnome didn't groan or cry out.

"Pathetic," Ferrao called out. "Your toys are nothing before true artifacts."

The corner near Maria exploded a second later,

knocking her back several feet. She brushed some rubble out of her hair and dust off her face, coughing.

"Damn it," the cop muttered. "How do we fight that? I'm not sure our anti-magic deflectors can take a direct hit from something like that."

Shay frowned. She'd forgotten to give Maria one of the rings, but she didn't have time to mess with it right then. They needed to take out Ferrao first.

She shouldered her rifle and twisted two rings on her hand, muttering a quick incantation in Latin. A white aura appeared around her.

She unsheathed her *tachi*. "I just need to get close to win….I think."

Maria's eyes widened. "You think?"

"Killing's an art, not a science." Shay shrugged.

"Killing's an art, not a science," Maria mimicked with a high-pitched mocking voice. "I hope that shit goes on your tomb—" Another blast blew out the wall and sent her flying into the wall behind her. Her head smacked against the wall, and she slumped to the floor.

"Maria!"

Ferrao laughed. "That's what happens when you won't come and face me, little human girls."

Shay stared wide-eyed at her friend, almost dropping the sword until she saw Maria's chest was still rising and falling.

Okay, she's just knocked out. Fine. I'll finish this bastard myself. Since the guy can obviously see even with the faceplate down, I'm just going to have to trust these damned artifacts.

"As I was saying earlier," Shay shouted, "men are men

no matter where they're from. Always overcompensating for small dicks."

"This is your idea of taunting me, human?" Ferrao snarled. "I'm older than most of your pathetic excuses for *countries*. You're an insect, maybe a cute pet at most."

Shay turned the corner, her hands gripping the hilt of the *tachi* tightly. "Am I supposed to be impressed? From what I can tell, Mr. Super Ancient, you've been having your ass handed to you—mostly by humans. I'd be pretty embarrassed if kittens kept kicking my ass."

Ferrao snorted and raised his arms, aiming the blast cannons right at her chest. "I've seen things you couldn't even imagine."

She rolled her eyes. "Is this the part where you talk about everything disappearing like tears in the rain?"

The gnome's face scrunched up in confusion. "Huh?"

"Look it up on the internet, asshole. Oh, you can't, because you'll be dead."

Ferrao blasted Shay. The orbs slammed into her, the heat warming her face, but the aura around her only brightening.

"Impossible," he yelled.

Shay laughed. "You really need to check out a dictionary if you're gonna keep saying that." She charged him.

The sword cut into the armor. Ferrao jumped back, his blood dripping on the ground. Shay didn't hesitate as she charged and brought the blade down on his arm. The *tachi* sliced through, and his armored limb flew to the ground, blood spraying all over the hall.

The gnome howled and shoved the other cannon into her stomach at point blank range. The following blast sent her into a wall, pain spiking through her entire body. The *tachi* fell to the tile.

"You insect," Ferrao shrieked. He fell to his knees, supporting himself with his remaining arm. "You worm. How dare you!"

Shay shook her head, trying to clear it. Her aura and rings had both vanished, and his blast had torn into her abdomen, giving her a nice view of her charred digestive tract. Every breath brought new agony. She pushed off the wall and snatched her sword from the ground.

"It's your fault," the tomb raider muttered through gritted teeth. "All you had to do if you didn't want me involved was not kidnap me." She channeled her pain into a scream and rushed toward the gnome. He brought up his cannon, but not in time. With a powerful swipe, she decapitated him.

Shay fell to her knees as the gnome's helmeted head bounced off a wall and landed with a clatter. She pulled out a healing potion and downed the contents. Her flesh restored itself.

After grabbing her weapon, she sheathed it and hurried over to check on Maria. Thin trails of blood ran down the cop's face. Shay pulled out another healing potion and forced it down the unconscious woman's throat.

The wounds healed, but she didn't wake up.

Damn it. Should have brought some energy potions, too.

"Guess you're just gonna have to sleep through the second half."

Shay glanced down the hall past the gnome's body.

If he was a Council member, then they probably have others going after James' and Trey's team.

She frowned, trying to decide who to reinforce, then, decision made, she ran down the hallway.

James arrived at a set of double doors, this time wood, but decorated with the same crest as the front doors. He kicked one off its hinges and rushed into the vast vehicle bay on the opposite side. Trucks, cars, helicopters, and VTOL aircraft were parked in the area, along with a few strange contraptions he assumed were Oriceran, including winged harnesses and ornithopters.

A distant whisper tickled his mind. He felt like he should know what it was, but he couldn't make it out.

Shay appeared around a truck with a smile. She tilted her head.

James frowned. "How did you get here so fast?"

"You know the world would be better off if you just gave up." She sighed. "And before you die, you should know that I don't love you. You're just a distraction, and I plan to leave you."

He blinked. "What the fuck?"

Heather walked out from behind the same truck. "It's your fault, you know."

"What the fuck are you talking about? How can you even be here? Wait, how the fuck are you *walking*?"

James grunted as he gazed at the two.

The faint whisper became more insistent, but he couldn't make it out. He was forgetting something important, but with Heather and Shay suddenly in front of him, it was hard to concentrate.

Heather pointed at him. "You think you saved me? Please. Now I work for the greatest monster of them all. The criminals don't avoid LA because of you. Is that what you thought? Nope. They come *because* you're there. To challenge you. You invite death. You're nothing more than a Horseman of the Apocalypse."

Shay nodded. "If I'd never met you, I'd have probably been satisfied with teaching at the school. Your bloodlust amplified my own. That's why I haven't been able to leave the violence behind."

A soft sigh came from behind him.

James spun to find Alison shaking her head.

What the fuck is going on?

Alison stared at him, eyes narrowed. "You're trying to turn me into you, Dad. A thug. A remorseless killer. My Drow side's going to overwhelm me and I'll become a monster, and it's all your fault. *Everything's* all your fault."

James stumbled backward. "What the fuck? How can you be here?" He frowned and growled. "Something... What?"

The three women surrounded him, pointing. "Sinner. *Failure*. You damage everything you touch. Monster. Thug. Freak."

Something clicked in the back of his mind, and he realized exactly who and what was in the room.

James roared in rage. "Fucking get them out of my mind." Agony struck his head, and he fell to his knees.

Link reestablished. Initiating thought filter.

The three women blurred, their forms replaced by hideous monsters. For a moment he thought they were despair bugs, but there were obvious differences—eight pairs of legs instead of six, the long body still segmented, but pale and fleshy instead of chitinous. Each was the same length, about ten feet, and rather than mandibles, their massive jaws were lined with several rows of sharp teeth. A single compound eye sat atop each of their heads.

James glared at each of the monsters, the pain in his head gone but his heart still thundering. "You fucking bastards. How fucking dare you pull that shit. I'm gonna tear you apart. You think you know fear and despair? I'll show you fucking despair."

Yes, the amulet whispered. *Anger hate. Power sufficient for advanced transformation.*

Silver-green tendrils shot from James' chest. This time the metallic bioarmor didn't stop with his chest and back. It moved all the way down his legs, ripping his pants in several places. A sort of helmet formed over his head, but despite his eyes being covered, he could see fine. Better than fine. His peripheral vision was wider. Both arms were tipped by blades, and his gauntleted hands now had claws.

His rifle clattered to the ground, and the armored bounty hunter advanced toward one of the monsters, growling under his breath. It charged, scuttling along the ground before launching itself at him. He gutted it by running a blade the length of its body. The monster body fell to the ground, and James finished it by slicing the head off.

The other two creatures backed up.

I will fucking rip you to shreds. You don't get in my fucking head.

The amulet was all but shouting in his mind. *Yes. Anger. Hate. Extended advanced transformation achieved.* Whispy

Doom's thought collapsed into pure bliss and murmurs of excitement.

James growled and pointed one arm at each creature on instinct. Sparks of green light played over the blades. More and more sparks flowed over the blades until a torrent of pure energy twisted and turned around each, accompanied by a growing crackle.

"Die, you motherfuckers!" he yelled.

Twin rays of intense green light blasted from the armor and tunneled through the monsters. Their bodies twitched for a few seconds before slumping to the ground.

James stood for a moment, his breathing labored.

Enemies defeated. Continue. Find additional enemies for adaptation. Grow stronger. Kill.

Yeah. Kill.

Trey hissed and downed a healing potion, then shook his head and looked at the wounded men lined up against the wall. No one was dead, but most had burned through their healing potions and could barely move from exhaustion. Piles of dead witches and wizards lay in the cafeteria that had become their battleground.

Fuck. Never gonna bitch about a boring bag and tag again.

Shorty wiped some blood out of his eyes. "This shit is fucking nasty, man. These fuckers are all fighting like they're high."

Guess we'd fight hard, too, if someone invaded Camp Brownstone.

Trey frowned and pointed at Shorty's neck. "Where's your deflector?"

Shorty looked down. "Guess it broke in those last attacks." He laughed. "Don't look at me like that. Yours is gone, too, Trey."

He glanced down. Shorty was right. Zoe's locket remained on his chest as well as the chain that had held the deflector, but the crystal was gone, probably shattered like so many others.

Trey walked over to a Council wizard who was bleeding out. His wand lay beside him, broken in half.

"Looks like we won, bitch."

The wizard coughed up blood. "So many of you are wounded. It'll take a while for the paralysis spells to wear off on the rest. It doesn't matter. The Council will finish them. You don't understand their power. We're apprentices compared to them."

Trey snorted. "I don't think you understand the power of James Motherfucking Brownstone, bitch."

The wizard laughed. "You won't survive anyway." He lifted his hand to his face. "You never could win."

"What the fuck are you talking about?"

"For the Council." The wizard grabbed a tooth and twisted it.

A bright flash blinded Trey.

"Shit."

Shorty rushed toward Trey and shoved him away "Look out, Tr—"

The wizard's body exploded, and the shockwave slammed both men into a nearby wall.

Trey groaned and shook his head, every muscle in his

body aching and his clothes shredded and burned. He grabbed his final healing potion and downed it. Zoe's locket turned pale blue and cracked.

He took a few deep breaths as the pain vanished and his wounds healed.

"Yo, Shorty, you all right? That shit was too close. If you hadn't pushed me out of the way, I might have taken a dangerous little nap."

No answer.

Trey swallowed and slowly turned his head. His friend and teammate lay against the wall, his head lolling to this side and his eyes staring straight ahead, glassy. His chest wasn't moving.

"No," Trey yelled. "Hell, no!" He crawled to his friend and took his pulse. Nothing. He shot to his feet and spun toward the wounded men on the side of the room. "Does anyone have a fucking healing potion left?"

Max pushed himself to his feet and hobbled toward him, potion in hand. "I thought I might need it later."

Trey ran to him and snatched the potion. He ran back over to Shorty and forced his mouth open before dumping the potion down his throat.

"Come on, you stupid son of a bitch," Trey muttered. "This ain't how you're supposed to go out. You talked about it, bitch. You have a motherfucking future now. You have to live."

The seconds ticked by with no change. Trey shoved Shorty on his back and started chest compressions. "Come *on*. Fight, damn you. Fucking fight. You're a bounty hunter for the Brownstone Agency. You don't give the fuck up until the big man gives you explicit fucking permission."

He kept up the CPR as every wounded man forced himself to his feet and made their way to them.

"It's no use," Lachlan whispered, tears leaking from his eyes. "You can't heal a dead man."

Trey threw his head back and howled in rage. "Shorty!"

24

James slammed through the doors out of the vehicle bay and continued down a hallway. Two wizards jumped from a side corridor and blasted him with fireballs, but he barely noticed the attack as he moved forward and cut them in half.

Whispy Doom kept alternating between flooding his mind with joy and encouraging him to seek the Council—not that he needed to be told. Anger fueled his movements.

The armored bounty hunter's steps echoed in the narrow hallway that opened into a vast high-ceilinged room filled with chairs. Some sort of assembly room, perhaps.

Tyler's briefings made the identity of the two people on the stage clear immediately—Crazak and Yilin.

The elf grinned and shook his head. "I see you have access to power we didn't anticipate, Mr. Brownstone. I would have loved to test you against some of the more exotic creatures we've been using, but it seems the PDA has finally figured out how to block the more special portals. Unfortunate."

James growled. "You're nothing. You're just a dead man walking. Shut your fucking mouth."

Crazak sneered. "Don't think because you've beaten a few of our minions that you can win against us." He raised his hand, and a firebolt ripped from it and struck James.

The bounty hunter growled, more out of irritation than pain.

Yilin thrust out her hands, and six ice lances struck James. They cracked against the armor, again barely noticeable.

Kill the Council. Defeat enemies. Grow stronger. Achieve mastery form.

James stalked toward Crazak. The rage from before remained there, burning, but the blinding rage that had taken him over during his last use of the armor was absent. The earlier emotions had been like an explosion, but this hatred and anger was like a sniper rifle aimed at the Council.

Crazak sneered. After a quick motion to draw an energy glyph in the air, a flowing blue force field popped in front of him.

The bounty hunter stomped right up to the field, and the field vanished with few quick slashes of his blade.

The elf backed up with a frown. James jerked his head to the side as a door closed. Yilin had fled.

She won't get away. I'll just kill her later.

Crazak stumbled back, more quick motions and incantations coming. A ball of void-black light appeared between his palms, and he laughed.

"I've wanted to test this for a while," the elf explained. "It wasn't worth the risk. You should be honored."

James shook his head. "You can't fucking win against me. Just lie down and die already."

The elf smirked. "Armor is nice, Mr. Brownstone, but it just protects from forces, magical or otherwise. This isn't a force. This is anti-life magic that has been tuned to better affect humans. Don't worry, after I kill you I'm sure I'll find some use for your nice artifact armor."

The black ball shot out and slammed into James. The blast knocked him into the air, and he flew back, crashing to the floor in the hallway.

Pain. Nothing but *pain.* He groaned and blinked, his vision hazy.

When his vision cleared after a few seconds, there was a massive hole in his chest armor, and he was pretty sure he could see his ribs.

Useful. New attack. New adaptation, potential strong.

James tried to take deep breaths, but his lungs wouldn't fill with air.

Can't you heal me? he thought.

Faster than normal rate insufficient for battle.

Crazak's laugh echoed throughout the room. "I'll grant you credit, Mr. Brownstone. The mere fact you survived that attack proves you're far more impressive than any others who would come against us. I'm tempted to believe that any other human on the planet would have died."

Probably right. Not a human, asshole. Fuck. Can't breathe.

James dug into a pouch with his claws and pulled out a healing potion. He ripped the stopper out with his teeth and downed the bottle. Seconds later, he could feel the pain ebbing. He downed an energy potion, then pulled out another healing potion.

Can't you fix the hole? he thought.

Severe damage, the amulet replied. *Adaptation achieved, but regeneration limited.*

Maybe this will help.

He poured the potion over the armor.

New adaptation, potential strong. Improved short-term regeneration, exterior and interior adaptation in progress.

The hole in the armor closed.

"If you crawl in here," Crazak called, "I'll make your death quick. Otherwise, I intend to take my time to teach you a lesson about daring to oppose the Council."

Healed, James stood and stepped back into the room.

Kill the enemy. Adaptation potential satisfied.

The bounty hunter took deep breaths. Killing wasn't good enough. He wanted to shred Crazak and make him pay. James might not have been out of control, but the anger and hate refused to leave. Every stray thought bounced back to punishing and destroying his enemy, and the amulet loved it.

James marched toward Crazak. "You could have avoided dealing with me, but you chose to target my city and my woman, so now you're gonna die. No mercy. No second chances. Just you fucking dying."

The elf snorted and summoned another black ball. The ball shot from his hands and smashed into James, the energy dissipating into the air with only a mild sting.

Crazak's eyes widened, and something delicious appeared on his face: fear.

A fireball came next, then a lightning bolt. The elf

conjured a sickly green orb of acid and flung it at James. The attacks stung but didn't slow the advancing juggernaut.

The elf jerked his head around. "Yilin! Where are you?"

"She left," James rumbled. He jumped from halfway across the room, his bioarmor-enhanced legs sending him flying. The bounty hunter landed with a loud thud right in front of Crazak, the wood of the stage cracking.

The mighty elf leader of the Council scrambled backward, his face showing his panic.

Not so tough now, huh?

James grunted and pierced his heart with a blade. He pulled the blade out and then sliced the elf's head off. Growling, he began hacking at the body, mindless anger now dominating him.

If he'd been paying more attention, he might have noticed the chill in the air right before the ice formed around his arms and legs. James fell to the ground, grunting. He thrashed and slammed his arms against the stage, but more ice formed around him until only his head was free of it.

Yilin laughed and clapped from the other side of the room. She made her way onto the stage and stood over James, smiling down at him. She stared at him with her solid-black eyes, a hint of amusement on her face.

James growled and thrashed, but it didn't accomplish anything.

Cold adaptation will maintain body functions, the amulet explained.

He ignored it and grunted. The frostling needed to die. They *all* needed to die.

Yilin sighed. "That's the problem. You might have taken out Crazak, but who had your back? This is why heroes die. They aren't cowardly enough."

"I've got his back," called a familiar voice. *Shay*.

Yilin spun and brought up an ice shield just in time to stop Shay from running her through. The frostling leapt backward. "Mere inconvenience."

"Except I've got *her* back," Maria called from the hallway, her rifle up. "Let's kill this bitch already. It's time to go home."

Yilin jerked her head toward the cop. Maria fired a burst, the anti-magic bullets nailing the frostling. The Oriceran hissed and waved her hand. A wall of ice formed in front of the door.

Shay's blade pierced Yilin's back and erupted from her chest. She leaned forward to whisper into her ear. "Shouldn't have let yourself get distracted. I guess we know who the real cold-blooded killer is." She yanked the blade out and pushed the body to the ground.

James stared up at Shay, her presence pushing back at the murderous rage that wanted to keep spilling out.

She tilted her head and smirked. "Huh, now it gives you a helmet, too? It doesn't look that cool, just so you know."

Get me the fuck out of here, James thought to the amulet.

Temporary realignment of temperature control in progress. Quiescence will follow due to extreme adaptation cycles.

The helmet receded along with the armor. His entire body warmed, and the ice melted into a puddle.

Shay laughed and walked over to him. "That hot to see me, huh?"

25

Shay helped James up, and they stared down at the dead Council members.

James grunted and shook his head. "That's two down. Two to go."

She shook her head. "Just one. Maria and I took out the gnome."

An explosion blasted a hole in the ice wall and the AET lieutenant rushed through, her rifle ready and her lips pursed.

"It's okay," Shay called from the stage. "We killed the two Council members. Just that last freaky one left."

James' phone rang, and he blinked and grabbed it out of his shredded pants pocket. The call was from Senator Johnston.

"Yeah?" he answered.

"Ah, good to hear your voice, son," came the cheery reply. "PDA just told me that big-ass shield around the facility went down, so I figured we'd be able to get in contact with you. I was hoping that means you'd finished the job."

"Three out of four. Just He Who Hunts left. Most of the minions have been cleaned up."

The senator chuckled. "Good, good. How are you and yours, son?"

"Beat up." James frowned. He had no idea how Trey's team had done. They might be facing He Who Hunts. "I've got to go. I need to find some of my guys."

"Fine," Senator Johnston replied. "Since the main defenses are down and you've thinned the ranks, we're going to send in some heavy-duty reinforcements. Don't worry about your pay. It'll be the same."

James grunted. "Fine. Do whatever you need to."

"Talk to you soon, son."

The call ended.

"The military's sending in a bunch of guys for final clean up. Won't affect our pay."

Shay shrugged. "I don't give a shit, then."

Maria stared down at the bodies of Crazak and Yilin. "Three out of four is good revenge. Let the Army finish off the last bastard."

Lachlan stumbled into the room, wincing in pain, and tears on his cheeks. "Big man, we've got bad trouble. Come with me."

James frowned. He'd seen the man injured seriously and not cry. Something had gone terribly wrong.

Lachlan rushed out of the room. James, Maria, and Shay hopped off the stage and sprinted after him. A few quick turns brought them to a scene of carnage, dead Council witches and wizards all over and the center of the room charred, a few limbs scattered. All of the Brownstone bounty hunters huddled at the other end of the room. Trey knelt, one arm against the wall, his face frozen in disbelief. Shorty lay on the ground.

James hurried over to Shorty. He'd seen enough dead bodies in his life to recognize one instantly.

Damn it. Damn it. Damn it.

"The government's sending troops to clean up," he murmured. "I'm sure they can get us out of here. We're fucking done."

Trey pushed off the wall. "Boys, help me carry him. He deserves some dignity for now."

Five men walked over to help Trey and they picked up the body, hoisting him over their shoulders. Pallbearers without a coffin.

The group marched, James in the lead, until they arrived at the blasted remains of the front doors. They stepped outside to helicopters and VTOL landing craft deploying soldiers.

An officer rushed up to James. "Mr. Brownstone, we've been ordered to evacuate your men. Do you have any wounded?"

The bounty hunter grunted. "Yeah. Several guys hurt." He nodded to Shorty. "We lost a man, and we need to guarantee his body gets back to LA."

The officer nodded. "I'm sorry for your loss, Mr. Brownstone." He frowned. "I know how it feels to lose good men on an operation."

James gritted his teeth. He didn't. At least he hadn't before. He'd been angry when cops got hurt, but those weren't *his* men.

I'm sorry, Shorty. If it makes any difference and God lets you watch down here at all, just know we gutted the fucking Council.

Two days later, Major Tennett and his SAS squadron surrounded the last warehouse in the Amsterdam headquarters of the Council. Other NATO Special Forces units, including American, French, Belgian, German, and Dutch forces, were contributing to Operation Cold Iron.

Everyone wanted the Council finished. The Americans had cleaned up most of the mess, but there was still one member of the Council at large, a mysterious being who went by "He Who Hunts."

You arrogant bloody bastard. How does it feel to be the hunted?

Two of his men set up breach charges on the door.

"Iron troop breaching in five," he transmitted. He tapped on his exoskeleton control panel to start the railgun's charging cycle.

The other units radioed their acknowledgment.

Five, four, three, two, one…

The breach charges blew open the door and the SAS soldiers rushed into the room, their exoskeletal feet clanking on the cold cement of the warehouse floor.

A cloaked figure, his head invisible under his hood except for his glowing red eyes floated several feet above crates filled with artifacts.

"Target sighted," shouted one of the men.

"Open fire!" the major shouted.

Bullets and railguns came to life, a dense cloud of

deadly projectiles filling the warehouse. The bullets and railguns shredded the cloak, but they didn't seem to be doing much other damage to its wearer. The Council member cackled with glee.

The major gritted his teeth. From what he'd been told He Who Hunts could be wounded, and the Americans had managed to do just that. All the Special Forces personnel for Operation Cold Iron were using anti-magic rounds, so he didn't know why the bastard wouldn't die.

Shuddering red tendrils of mist emerged from the robe and lifted into the air. A few seconds later, reddish-blue bolts blasted from them and struck a half-dozen soldiers. Some were hit in their heads, others their chests or legs. The effects were the same: their afflicted body parts melted like ice hit by a blowtorch.

Screams ripped from the throats of the soldiers not killed instantly.

"This is Iron 1. Withdraw. Withdraw. All Merlins enter and engage. I repeat, all Merlins enter and engage."

The soldiers kept up their fire as they backed toward the doors. Orbs, rays, and bolts blasted from all sides now as a huge force of witches and wizards entered. They included people from a variety of agencies, including America's Paranormal Defense Agency and the United Kingdom's Ministry of Mystical Security. A thin invisible shield absorbed some of the hits, but many were blowing past it and striking He Who Hunts.

Glowing green ichor spewed from the mist creature now. He might have developed an immunity to bullets, even anti-magic bullets, but raw magic from dozens of witches and wizards was not so easily ignored.

He Who Hunts jerked and twitched, more and more of his robe burning away, revealing the swirling mass of gaseous red beneath. Ichor dripped from it. A misty tentacle snatched a small hand mirror from a nearby crate.

The creature threw it on the ground, the sound of the smashing glass swallowed by the din of the spells being flung at him.

A jagged crack of light in the air appeared above the mirror, blinding in its intensity. The major squinted and looked away, the filters on his helmet not doing much to help. The light died, and the last scrap of He Who Hunts' robe disappeared into the crack. The fissure in reality sealed itself behind him.

Major Tennett frowned. "This is Iron 1. Cease fire. Cease fire. Target has fled."

A few seconds passed before the mages stopped their attack. He sighed and headed back into the warehouse to look around. Crates filled with artifacts littered the place. He recognized several from a briefing about the LA museum raid.

The enemy might have escaped, but the bastard had lost his last major base and all his artifacts.

Whatever the hell you are, what was your plan?

Major Tennett shook his head. His mission was over. He'd leave the enigma for someone else.

James kept his hands folded in front of him, just staring straight ahead at Shorty's coffin at the front of the church. He'd never been to this particular church, given that they were African Methodist Episcopal rather than Catholic, but it didn't look so different from his church.

God's house is God's house, I guess. Just a different paint job.

The pews were filled with people, including every man from the Brownstone Agency and Royce, and most of their families. Shay sat beside him.

Several police officers in full dress uniform lined the back, including Sergeant Mack and Lieutenant Hall. Trey sat between Charlyce and Nana Garfield, a solemn look on his face. Father McCartney was there, even though he wasn't participating in the service in a formal capacity.

The pastor finished a prayer at the front. "I would like to take this time for any in the community to speak about Brother Theo."

James almost chuckled. Shorty seemed more like his real name than Theo.

Nana Garfield raised her hand.

"Please, sister," the pastor replied. "Feel free to stand where you are and share your story."

She stood and cleared her throat. "We all know what we used to think about Theo. We used to think, 'That boy is up to no good. Nothing but trouble, running the streets, thinking about being a thug and a gangster.'"

Several people nodded, and James frowned.

It's his funeral. Come on.

The old woman pointed at the coffin. "But he didn't die no gangster, now did he? Y'all have seen it on the news. Terrorists. Terrorists with unholy magic straight from hell. He died a hero fighting them. That boy didn't need to be there. He didn't need to be doing what he was doing, risking his life to go after criminals. But he changed. He took the strength he wanted to use to prove himself on the streets, and he used it to help others. The Lord chose to take him from us at a young age, and it can be hard to understand His plan at times, but think about this. Who knows what would have happened if those awful Council people had gotten away with it? How many people did Theo save with his sacrifice? May he find peace with the Lord in heaven."

Several people murmured and nodded their agreement, sprinkles of "amen" following.

James looked down and took a deep breath.

Shay reached over to squeeze James' hand, a soft look on her face.

Community member after community member rose to offer their condolences and thoughts. All gave variations on what Nana Garfield had offered. They'd thought he was shifty and useless, but he'd turned his life around, and they couldn't be prouder of the fact that he had died to help take down evil people.

Trey stood to offer his piece. "Y'all can keep calling him Theo, but he'll always be Shorty to me. I've known him for a long time. When we were no-good thugs, sometimes we ran together, sometimes we didn't. I was worried for a while we were going end up in wrong…groups together, if you know what I'm saying."

Everyone laughed.

"I didn't know what was gonna happen when he tried to join the Brownstone Agency. I thought, 'You didn't want to run with my boys before, but now you do?'" He blinked his eyes, a few tears leaking out. "We was just talking, not all that long ago, about the future, you know? About how he used to think there was no future for him, but everything changed because his life had turned around." He took a deep breath and looked up at a cross on the wall. "I'm not one to question the Ultimate Big Man, and y'all are right. Shorty might have died too soon, but he died stopping terrible, terrible people and saving my life. I hope everyone in this neighborhood understands what Shorty represents: redemption and second chances, you know what I'm saying?"

Everyone nodded, with more than a few "uh huhs" coming out of the crowd.

"We all make mistakes. We all march the wrong path on some days. We all let ourselves think the Devil's got a better benefits package sometimes, and it tempts us, but as long as we remember that there's always hope, we can turn it around and become something better than we have been." Trey pulled a handkerchief out of his suit to wipe his eyes and sat. "I miss you already, brother. I'll make sure there's a good future for everyone, so it wasn't a waste."

Several people patted him on the shoulder.

Charlyce stood, tears streaming down her face. She opened her mouth in song.

"Amazing grace, how sweet the sound."

Everyone joined in the next line. James remained silent.

"That saved a wretch like me.
I once was lost, but now am found,
Was blind, but now I see.
Twas grace that taught my heart to fear,
And grace my fears relieved.
Twas grace that taught my heart to fear,
And grace my fears relieved,

How precious did that grace appear
The hour I first believed!
Amazing grace, how sweet the sound.
This time James joined in, his voice low and rumbling.
That saved a wretch like me.
I once was lost, but now am found,
Was blind, but now I see."

James sat under a tree, his hands behind his head as he watched everyone chat at the post-funeral barbeque. Despite the dark clothes and somber occasion, people smiled, trading their stories of the man Shorty had become, not the man he'd once been.

As for Shorty's boss, he just needed a little quiet. He'd even asked Shay to leave him alone with his thoughts for a few minutes.

Shit's different now. It's not just Leeroy and me. I've built something, and I have responsibilities to not just my men, but to the community.

He looked up at the sky.

Have I done the right thing? I'm not gonna pretend I'm a good man, but I'm trying to do well by those around me.

James took a deep breath and nodded. Part of love is the pain of loss. He'd known that from a young age. He'd lost his parents and his foster father. The super-despair bugs—or whatever the hell those things in Wyoming had been—had tried to play on that.

No. Never again. I opened up a little bit, and it's turning me into a better man. I could have been giving to the community for years, helping people do something better, instead of lying to myself that ignoring everyone else was for the best.

An earlier conversation with Lachlan floated up.

Just saying, big man, that you could have been one of those high-level guys you hunt. You could have busted up banks like King Pyro or killed like that crazy bitch at the farmer's market. But you ain't doing that shit, even though everyone knows you're the baddest motherfucker in America."

James grunted. He wasn't a piece of trash only because of the people around him who had cared. Now it was time to do what he could to pay those people back by helping others.

Shorty had decent savings. No one even knew where his deadbeat parents were, so on Trey's advice, James had had his lawyer prepare paperwork to make sure Shorty's savings would go to his two teenage cousins who still lived in the neighborhood.

One of them, Jerome, walked toward James after finishing a plate of ribs. The bounty hunter stood and offered the boy a polite nod.

Jerome grinned.

"What's so funny?" James rumbled.

"It's just you. You're a livin' legend. I ain't see Shorty much after he started workin' for you, but every time I did see him, he was less trashy." He shrugged.

James shook his head. "He was never trash. He just needed someone to give him a real chance."

The boy looked down for a moment before looking up and nodding. "When I graduate, I'm joining the Army. I want to help defend the country like Shorty did. Gonna train up and do my time, and after that, maybe I'll be good enough to join the Brownstone Agency."

James smiled. "Yeah, kid, maybe you will. See you in a few years, then."

"See you, Mr. Brownstone." The boy waved and walked off.

James sat again, and his thoughts drifted for a few minutes.

Father McCartney, who had been chatting with the pastor, looked James' way. The priest murmured something to the other man and rose to make his way over to James' not-so-hidden spot.

"Care for a little confessional outside the box?" the priest asked.

James shrugged. "Ashes to ashes and all that. Death just makes a man think."

The priest sat beside him. "About what?"

"If a man's leaving a good mark on the world."

Father McCartney smiled. "And what do you think?"

James sighed. "I think I'm beginning to get there, but I have a long way to go. Maybe won't even get there before I die, but I still want to walk the road."

The priest chuckled. "It heartens me to hear you say that. It means you must have at least been paying a little attention during my sermons."

"I always pay attention. Paying attention and understanding are two separate things."

Father McCartney stared at him for a moment. "You're a good man, James Brownstone. Yes, we're all sinners, but we can still be good men and women. That's what His sacrifice was all about."

James rubbed the back of his neck. "I'll try and keep that in mind."

The priest stood and pulled on the bottom of his shirt to straighten it. "If you ever need me, you know where to find me." He turned to leave, then stopped. Without turning back around, he smiled. "By the way, the next time you decide to send an anonymous donation, just give it straight to me. I'll never refuse you again."

Father McCartney walked off.

James watched the priest make his way back to the tables.

He isn't just saying something to me to make me feel better. If he's willing to accept my money no matter what, he really does *feel I'm a good man.*

James nodded. It was a small triumph, but enough to make him feel good about his profession, pain and all.

EPILOGUE

Senator Johnston sipped his coffee. Galahad sat across from him with a frown on his face.

"Oh, don't look so sour, son. The good guys won this time." The senator shrugged. "Even if we didn't get the last bastard, his organization's done, and we recovered all the artifacts. The Council is as dead as disco."

Galahad shrugged. "I'm less worried about that than the hackers I leaked the information to."

"Why is that? I *wanted* them to have the information."

"Because I can't figure out how they did it. The whole point of how I set it up was to make sure I could tag them at the end. They got into the system somehow, but I couldn't tag them." Galahad shook his head. "*No one's* that good."

Senator Johnston smiled. "Apparently, someone is. Don't worry. This situation's under control from several angles."

Galahad's watch buzzed, and he stood. "I need to go."

The senator smiled and lifted his coffee cup. "Thanks again for all your help, son."

The hacker hurried out and Senator Johnston relaxed, taking the time to enjoy his coffee.

About five minutes later, he threw a few bills on the table and made his way outside to a large waiting SUV.

A suited man opened the door from the inside, and the senator took a seat.

"Everything okay, sir?" the man asked.

Senator Johnston nodded. "Fine, son. Just someone who doesn't like to be beaten." He chuckled. "Poor boy can't figure out how they did it."

"Well, sir, neither can we."

The older man grinned. "Still a few mysteries in life, huh?"

The younger man sighed. "There was definitely magic involved, but the only thing the investigators found was a hole that was no more than a few inches high. Not large enough for even a decent microdrone to fit through." He frowned. "And there's one more strange thing."

"What's that?"

The other man glanced to the side, an embarrassed look on his face. "They found little orange circles on the ceiling and tested them. A lot of the results were inconclusive, but they identified several substances, including a dye, that are ingredients in a food product."

Senator Johnston arched a brow. "A food product?"

"Again, some inconclusive results, but most of the substances we could identify are found in Cheetos."

The senator laughed. "Cheetos?" He slapped a hand on

his knee and shook his head. “Collect the evidence you have. I want to send it to some people I know.”

Maybe if I push you a little, you’ll reveal your little trick. Galahad’s right. You’re on our side for now, but we can’t be sure you will be forever.

FINIS

AUTHOR NOTES - MICHAEL ANDERLE

SEPTEMBER 6, 2018

Before I explain what is going on, let me say THANK YOU for not only reading this book but these *Author Notes* as well!

Today is Sunday, and I'm working out of a new Mexican restaurant (Chavela's) in Henderson, NV (If you look east from the strip towards the mountains, I'm over there.)

LMBPN has set this BHAG (big hairy audacious goal) of releasing four hundred titles next year. To make this happen, we had to get cracking and bang a few brain cells together to figure out how to streamline our process.

Which, you know, was probably said last year, but I didn't FEEL like being responsible last year. As the owner of this company, I didn't want to be told when I had to have stories in. The whole concept made the obstinate part of my personality stand up and try to figure out who to flip off. (Editor's note: HAHAHAHAHAHAHA! Serves you right.)

In the end, I had to give myself the finger.

Way to fuck yourself over, Michael.

Why? Because it's one thing to have two or three (at most) books coming out in a week. But, when we started doing full weeks of books (well, five days, not weekends) the challenges exposed themselves.

One of the issues is fan pricing. How do we continue the pricing while reducing the effort? With four hundred books we have a LOT more to do, and emails are a serious time and effort suck. We already send too many.

FAN PRICING ON SATURDAYS

We are moving to releasing our books at $3.99 (a $1.00 less than regular price) during the week, then on Saturdays pricing all new releases (except box sets) at $0.99 for that day only. On Sunday, they go up to regular price.

This way you always know what day to look, and we are able to send two emails during the week focused on book releases. One on Sunday / Monday that announces what books are coming out (and when) for those who (for whatever reason) care, and then again on Saturday with the books and the links to the Amazon website (we don't always have these a week before.)

We are HOPING to put more content on the LMBPN Publishing website about interesting stuff that might apply to you (including games, Anime, backstory on stories and authors, etc.) When we get this working, we will start releasing a special Wednesday email to highlight our blog posts.

[Note from Steve: We're starting to post new content

already. If you haven't checked out the site, please do so, www.lmbpn.com]

Soon, I will be reducing my *Author Notes* in the back of collaboration books. There is no freaking way I can put out five-hundred-word (or more) *Author Notes* in the back of four hundred books. So, my plan is to do a Mad-Libs sort of deal where the core is consistent, and I can add in one or two unique items and see how that goes.

Making 2019 happen at four hundred books is a mountain-type goal for me. I suspect in 2020 we will reduce the number of books released as we use what we learned in 2019 to cut the chaff.

However, for those who follow us, we appreciate your shouts of encouragement as we try to accomplish something (to my knowledge) NO Indie Publishing Company is doing.

Bring it on, 2019, bring it on!

Ad Aeternitatem,

Michael Anderle

P.S. – We are planning for *The Unbelievable Mr. Brownstone* to go to eighteen books at this time, and Alison Brownstone, Inc. will be starting Winter 2018. Her stories will include her Dad of course, *and her Mom (grin) from time to time—but SHE is the focus.*

What will the criminals think when Alison, straight out of college, decides to take up the family business?

—

The man struggled. The rocks from the alley's cement ground into his side as the magical ropes circled around him. Every time he moved the ropes tightened, and it was starting to hamper his breathing. He stopped wriggling and looked up at the young woman who could not be more than twenty-two, yet had white hair. "Who ARE you?" he sputtered.

The woman smirked and knelt, patting him on the head before she spoke.

"I'm Alison Brownstone, bitch!"

OTHER REVELATION OF ORICERAN UNIVERSE BOOKS

The Unbelievable Mr. Brownstone

*** Michael Anderle ***

Feared by Hell (1) - Rejected by Heaven (2) - Eye For An Eye (3) - Bring the Pain (4) - She is the Widow Maker (5) - When Angels Cry (6) - Fire with Fire (7) - Hail To The King (8) - Alison Brownstone (9) - One Bad Decision (10) - Fatal Mistake (11)

I Fear No Evil

*** Martha Carr and Michael Anderle ***

Kill the Willing (1) - Bury the Past, But Shoot it First (2) - Reload Faster (3) - Dead In Plain sight (4) - Tomb Raiding PHD (5) - Tomb Raider Emeritus (6)

School of Necessary Magic

*** Judith Berens ***

Dark Is Her Nature (1) Bright Is Her Sight (2) - Wary Is Her Love (3) - Strong Is Her Hope (4)

Rewriting Justice

*** Martha Carr and Michael Anderle ***

Justice Served Cold (1) - Vengeance Served Hot (2) - Bounty Hunter Inc (03)

The Leira Chronicles

*** Martha Carr and Michael Anderle ***

Waking Magic (1) - Release of Magic (2) - Protection of Magic (3) - Rule of Magic (4) - Dealing in Magic (5) - Theft of Magic (6) - Enemies of Magic (7) - Guardians of Magic (8)

The Soul Stone Mage Series

*** Sarah Noffke and Martha Carr ***

House of Enchanted (1) - The Dark Forest (2) - Mountain of Truth (3) - Land of Terran (4) - New Egypt (5) - Lancothy (6) - Virgo (7)

The Kacy Chronicles

*** A.L. Knorr and Martha Carr ***

Descendant (1) - Ascendant (2) - Combatant (3) - Transcendent (4)

The Midwest Magic Chronicles

*** Flint Maxwell and Martha Carr***

The Midwest Witch (1) - The Midwest Wanderer (2) - The Midwest Whisperer (3) - The Midwest War (4)

The Fairhaven Chronicles

*** with S.M. Boyce ***

Glow (1) - Shimmer (2) - Ember (3) - Nightfall (4)

BOOKS BY MICHAEL ANDERLE

For a complete list of books by Michael Anderle, please visit

www.lmbpn.com/ma-books/

All LMBPN Audiobooks are Available at Audible.com and iTunes. For a complete list of audiobooks visit:

www.lmbpn.com/audible

CONNECT WITH MICHAEL ANDERLE

Michael Anderle Social

Website:

http://kurtherianbooks.com/

Email List:

http://kurtherianbooks.com/email-list/

Facebook Here:

https://www.facebook.com/OriceranUniverse/

https://www.
facebook.com/TheKurtherianGambitBooks/

www.ingramcontent.com/pod-product-compliance
Lightning Source LLC
Chambersburg PA
CBHW050230110726
47898CB00007B/2098

* 9 7 8 1 6 4 2 0 2 2 0 3 2 *